"You can't waste the last few hours of the year watching a football game," Lauren teased, kissing Maris on the cheek. "And I really could use a nap. But I think I'll take that long, hot bath instead."

Maris grinned as Lauren slid off of the bed. She sipped her beer until she heard the water running, then finished it in one long swallow before she jumped to her feet. After kicking off her boots, her fingers flew across the buttons on her blouse and the zipper on her jeans. Discarding her underwear on the floor, she took another beer out of the cooler and quietly walked to the partially opened bathroom door.

Lauren stood naked before the mirror and brushed her shoulder-length red hair. She twisted it into a knot and secured it with a rubber band. Leaning over the tub, she poured bubble bath into the water. A light floral fragrance filled the room as the bubbles formed. As she turned toward the tub, Maris sprang through the door, stepped over the side and dropped into the water. Startled, Lauren screamed and dropped the hotel soap.

"Goddamn, this water is hot," Maris said, leaning over to put the unopened beer on their porcelain table.

"Serves you right if you burn your ass. You almost gave me a heart attack. I thought you were watching football."

"I decided to join you instead."

"You could have asked first. If you had given me a chance, I might have invited you."

About the Author

Kaye Davis is a criminalist in a Texas Department of Public Safety regional crime laboratory with nineteen years experience. Her areas of expertise include the analysis of drugs, the examination of paint samples and the comparison of shoeprint and tire track evidence. She has testified in court over three hundred times and has participated in numerous crime scene investigations.

Kaye is a native Texan and lives in the Dallas area with her partner of seventeen years and two dogs, Trooper and Dispatcher. Her first novel, *Devil's Leg Crossing*, (the 1st Maris Middleton Mystery) was published in 1997 by Naiad Press.

POSSESSIONS

THE 2ND MARIS MIDDLETON MYSTERY

BY KAYE DAVIS

THE NAIAD PRESS, INC.
1998

Printed in the United States of America on acid-free paper
First Edition

Editor: Christine Cassidy
Cover designer: Bonnie Liss (Phoenix Graphics)
Typesetter: Sandi Stancil

Library of Congress Cataloging-in-Publication Data

Davis, Kaye, 1956 –
    Possessions : a Maris Middleton mystery / by Kaye Davis.
        p.   cm.
    ISBN 1-56280-192-9 (pbk.)
    1. Lesbians — Fiction   I. Title.
PS3554.A934925P67   1998
813'.54—dc21   97-40375
                                                            CIP

To
Mother and Daddy
and
Karolyn and Kelly

Acknowledgments

My deepest thanks to Felicia Farias, who helped read and organize the final draft; Kenneth Evans, who helped with last-minute research; and Lorna Beasley, who patiently answered my DNA questions.

Special thanks to my editor, Christine Cassidy, for all of her excellent advice.

And to Lynda Ann . . . for everything.

Chapter One

Maris stopped her pacing and peered through the sliding glass door separating her laboratory from the rest of the duplex. She watched as Earnhardt, her border collie, danced excitedly around two straining movers as they struggled with another shipping crate. How many clothes did Lauren have, she wondered. Stepping away from the door, she turned her attention to the small white envelope and the package resting on the black-topped laboratory counter. She picked up the invitation, glanced at it and tossed it down. Next to it, with the brown packing tape neatly slit and the flaps pulled back, lay a brown cardboard box. It had been shipped UPS with a "groundtrac" bar-coded sticker attached to it next to a neatly typed mailing label addressed to *Middleton Forensic Services.* A sharp-toed, black patent right shoe with a three-inch heel rested inside. It was a size seven, B width, Lovelady's brand, with slight heel and sole wear. She noticed a yellowish stain on the inner liner.

A note that accompanied the shoe lay on the counter next to the open box. Maris read once more —*I KNOW WHO AND WHAT YOU ARE. STAY AWAY.* Handwritten in blue ink using large capital letters, the message was carefully centered in the middle of a yellow page of legal-sized paper. After donning latex gloves, Maris fingerprinted the shoe and the box. The outside of the box, not surprisingly, was covered with fingerprints, but none were detected on the black heel.

Although unsure of who sent the items and why, Maris understood the timing. On December twenty-first, she assisted in a crime scene investigation in Pierce, a rural county in East Texas, where a woman's body had been discovered in the drainage ditch on an isolated farm road. She was later identified as Theresa Eastin, a Dallas legal secretary kidnapped the Friday after Thanksgiving. The partially clad body was arranged in a sexually suggestive position that drew immediate attention to her mutilated genitalia. She was minus a left hand, severed at the wrist. Shiny red fingernail polish decorated her right hand. An expensive black shoe present on her left foot sported a two-inch heel, but the right shoe was absent. After the removal of the body, Chief Deputy Ralph Lambert, Texas Ranger Wayne Coffey and Maris, with the help of several Pierce county deputies, scoured the area for evidence but found nothing of importance. Someone close to the investigation had leaked descriptions of the missing hand to the press despite repeated warnings from Ralph and Wayne. But as far as Maris knew, no public information had been released about the missing shoe.

Spirited barking brought her back to the glass door. Lauren, propping a hand on her hip, glared at Maris and tossed her dark red hair. Her green eyes flashed angrily as she crooked her finger, beckoning her. "Do something with your dog," she said, pointing at Earnhardt.

"Come here, boy." The movers struggled with a fourth shipping crate as Lauren pushed the furniture back to increase the floor space. "She's beautiful when she's aggravated, isn't she?" He whined and crouched alertly at the sliding door. Maris's own reflection in the door caught her eye. At five feet, ten inches, she was taller than Lauren and more muscular in build with dark brown hair and blue eyes. She thought the recent scar that ran down her right cheek from the corner of her eye to her jaw line added an air of mystery to her appearance and she liked it — much to her mother's distress.

Watching Lauren reminded her of the invitation to the New Year's Eve party only four days away in Austin — she'd waited apprehensively for it to arrive, half hoping they'd decided not to have it. Since it was late, she thought she might get her wish, but it had been sent to her old address first. When Mary Ann was alive, they had considered the annual party a respite after the hectic Christmas season full of family obligations and welcomed the excuse to slip

3

out of town and spend time together. They missed it last year for the first time because of Mary Ann's illness.

Maris sighed. It was hard to believe that Mary Ann had been dead for almost a year. There had been so many changes. She had started a forensic consulting business and opened a private lab. In September, Lauren, on a leave of absence from the FBI, came into her life when she asked for Maris's help in finding her missing sixteen-year-old niece. Unfortunately, their search ended when her niece was found dead. Once the investigation was complete, Lauren returned to active duty in Chicago. They were struggling to maintain a long-distance relationship when there was an unexpected opening in the Dallas regional FBI office. Lauren transferred, arriving the week before Christmas, a time of mixed emotions for Maris since it was her first without Mary Ann and her first with Lauren. With the added tension of introducing a new lover to the family, she bordered on total panic, but Lauren, calm, collected and charming, said the right things at the right time. Maris's father fell in love with her and Maris's sister and mother could think of nothing bad to say about her. Was it fair to subject Lauren to her friends so soon after the family? On another major holiday? Or maybe it was she, not Lauren, who wasn't ready?

"Hush, Earnhardt," Maris said, squatting to hug him. Three smaller boxes balanced precariously on top of one of the crates. Amazing, Maris thought, she had left all her furniture with her ex-husband but still required a Freightline hauler just to ship her clothes, shoes and personal items. Lauren signed the work order and dismissed the movers. She wore faded

4

jeans and Maris's favorite Dale Earnhardt NASCAR T-shirt. It was too big and hung halfway to her knees. Maris smiled as Lauren pulled her red hair, damp with sweat, away from her neck and snapped it into a loose ponytail with a rubber band.

Earnhardt scratched at the door and Maris opened it. He danced around Lauren's feet as she deftly slashed the top of a box with a kitchen butcher knife. Maris turned away. She needed to catch up on the analyses of the drug cases submitted over Christmas and scolded herself for wasting time. Several blood tubes, samples from the Christmas drunks arrested over the holidays, awaited testing for alcohol content. But the black heel haunted and intrigued her.

Taking the folder on Theresa Eastin out of the filing cabinet, she thumbed through the crime scene photos. The body was in bad shape, having ripened quickly in the warmer-than-normal December weather. There had been some carnivore and insect activity. When she came to the autopsy pictures, she dropped onto her stool. She had attended only one autopsy when she worked as a criminalist for the Texas Department of Public Safety. Since she'd opened her own lab, it had become a regular practice and not one she particularly enjoyed. The findings on this one were brutal, even to read, and the autopsy photos were worse. Theresa's torn clothing, when carefully removed, revealed the horrors her attacker had inflicted on her battered body. One picture documented a jagged wound of an unknown origin on her right side. Bite marks covered her chest and back. One breast was slashed and the nipple on the other hung by a thread. Vaginal mutilation was extreme. Nume-

5

rous cuts, some beginning to heal, marred her inner thighs and stomach. Ligature marks encircled her neck, wrists and ankles. Bruises, an odd rainbow of blue, yellow and black, covered her body. Her agony had lasted for days. Death, when it finally came, must have been merciful, Maris thought, closing the folder.

The Tyler pathologist, Dr. Henry Rodriguez, was convinced that most of the mutilation to the breasts and the vaginal area was postmortem. Maris hoped he was right. Death was due to strangulation after, at best estimate, two weeks of torture. Both the doctor and Maris believed that the body and clothing had been washed to remove any trace evidence. The dirt and stains on her clothing seemed to be consistent with decomposition and the filth in the drainage ditch. There was some evidence that the body may have been in cold storage for a while before it was dumped.

This was the first major criminal investigation since the Pierce County Sheriff's Department had signed a contract with Maris for forensic services. The deal had been approved over vigorous objections by one of the county commissioners and Maris was eager to jump into the case and prove her worth. So starting immediately on December twenty-second, the day after the autopsy, Maris had examined the samples from Theresa's clothing and hair combings for the presence of foreign hair, fibers, paint, semen — anything to help determine what happened to her and to prosecute the bastard who did it. Numerous spermatozoa were present on the smear the

6

pathologist made from the cervical mucus, and she thought there was enough present for DNA testing. Three short brown human hair fragments were found on her blouse and white cotton fibers were detected on the clothing and in her hair, indicating that the suspect had wrapped her body in a white sheet to transport it.

She searched through the box with Theresa Eastin's clothing until she located the sack with her remaining left shoe and held it side by side with the one she received from UPS. The brand, style and size were wrong. It was not the missing mate to Theresa's left shoe. She repackaged the Eastin evidence and locked it in the vault.

The note drew her attention. Grabbing a flashlight from a nearby drawer, she clicked off the lights in the lab and studied the surface of the note using oblique lighting. She saw slight indentations on the surface of the paper. It was not unusual, when someone wrote on the top sheet of a notepad, to leave impressions and, sometimes, traces of the ink on the surface of the next page. It is often possible to visualize these and occasionally decipher the message written on the missing previous page. Maris flipped on the light switch. Holding the note by one corner, she made a photocopy before placing the original in a manila folder that she slid gently into a large envelope.

She couldn't figure out what the message and shoe meant. Was it a practical joke? Possibly, but she doubted it. The newspaper leak told of the missing left hand but said nothing about the missing right shoe. The humor was too mild for one of her sick law enforcement buddies. If it was one of them, they'd have sent one of those battery-powered plastic hands rigged to move when she opened the box and scare the hell out of her.

Thinking Texas Ranger Wayne Coffey might have some ideas, she called his office. The Highway Patrol secretary in Pierce took his messages for him, and as soon as she answered Maris remembered that he was hunting mountain lions in Colorado until after the first of the year. Ralph and Sheriff Sizemore were with him. It was the first time Wayne's son got to go with them, and the boy had been very excited.

Thinking about the indentations in the note, Maris dialed another number. When a woman answered, she said, "Is this the beautiful and world famous Shannon Maria Stockwell?"

There was a moment of silence and then sparkling laughter filled Maris's ear. Shannon replied, "Maris Middleton, whatever it is the answer is no. The last time you called me I ended up in Detroit for two weeks during the middle of the worst blizzard in history."

"True, but that case got you on CNN. How many other questioned document examiners have had that privilege? I really called to ask you to run away for New Year's, but now you've hurt my feelings. Instead, how about letting me use some of your equipment and expertise?"

In a Mae West imitation containing the trace of a Texas drawl, Shannon said, "You can use my equipment anytime."

Maris laughed. "I need you to enhance the indentations on a sheet of yellow legal paper. It's im-

8

portant, possibly related to the rape-murder in Pierce county. The proposition is — I'll pay you when I get paid."

"I guess I owe you a favor. I made a lot of money off of the Detroit case even if I did freeze my ass off. Bring it over soon as you can."

After hanging up, Maris drummed her fingers on the lab counter. "What are you missing here?" she whispered. Obviously the victim's left hand and right shoe held a special meaning to the killer. He either took them as a trophy or souvenir or he had a sexual attachment — a fetish — for them. Wedding rings, the symbol of love and commitment, were traditionally worn on the left hand. Maybe that had some sick significance to him. Maybe specifically he was attracted to the victim by her painted nails and the black high-heeled shoes. If she assumed the warning on the note was real, either from Theresa Eastin's killer or another sicko, the shoe might be part of an erotic game. She could imagine the sender masturbating with the shoe and then, with perverse pleasure, mailing it to her. That might explain the yellow stain. Well, in a little more than a New York minute, she could answer that question.

Using the standard presumptive test for the presence of semen, Maris detected acid phosphatase, a constituent of seminal fluid, on the inside of the shoe. Using a scalpel, she cut out the inner liner and extracted it. She placed a portion of the extract on a slide and stained it with a dye. Examining it under the microscope, she found enough intact spermatozoa to perform DNA analysis on this sample and the one recovered from Theresa Eastin's body to determine if they were from the same man, but she hesitated to

9

use up the limited amounts available for testing until a suspect was apprehended. She decided to preserve a frozen stain from the shoe and decide later whether to run DNA. She stored the shoe and her reagents, removed her gloves and washed her hands.

Earnhardt bounced off of her leg and barked happily when she entered the living room. "Hush, fellow," she said. She picked up a black party dress lying on top of one of the shipping crates. She grinned. Lauren must be a sight to see in this one. She dropped it when Lauren returned to the room.

"What's wrong with him?" Lauren asked, grabbing another load of clothes to take to the back closet.

"Oh, he's just being his obsessive little border collie self." Maris followed her with an armful of clothing. Glancing into the middle bedroom, her junk room, she noticed Lauren had already appropriated it for her excess clothes and shoes. She realized why as she stared in amazement at the rows of shoes in the closet. Dozens of different styles and colors hid the floor. Boxes, stacked five deep, lined the back wall. "Honey, how many pairs of shoes do you have?" she asked. "I've never seen anyone with so many shoes."

"Anyone would have more than you, Maris. What do you have now? A pair of work boots, pair of dress boots and pair of athletic shoes. The homeless have more than you."

"I can only wear one pair at a time," Maris called out as she brought the last load of hanging clothes and dropped them on the bed next to Lauren.

She ignored them and looked up at Maris. "What's going on here? You're as anxious as Earnhardt." She caught Maris's hand. "If you don't want me to move in, tell me now." Maris heard the catch in her voice.

Angry at herself and feeling silly, she wrapped her arms around Lauren. "You're damned right I want you to move in here. One of the happiest days of my life was when I came home and found you on my porch, back from Chicago."

"I thought you wanted this, but you've been so distant today. You . . . and Earnhardt act like I'm an occupying army."

Maris laughed. "We've made love every night and most mornings since you returned. Do you really think I wouldn't want you to move in here?"

"I don't know. Something's wrong."

"Well, worry no more, my dear." She paused and added in a more serious voice, "It's not you, but January may be a hard month for me."

"Mary Ann . . . I should have guessed."

Maris didn't want to talk about it. Instead she asked, "If I were to invite you to a New Year's Eve party in Austin, which of these clothes would you wear?"

"Oh, I don't know. What do you think I should wear?"

"Not a fair question, I don't know what my choices are."

"Help me unload that last crate and you can help me decide. Maybe this one?"

She held up a beautiful teal silk suit and Maris felt her heart drop. "No, not that one," she said quickly.

"I thought you liked this color."

"I do," she said, fighting to hide her emotions,

"but I want to see my other choices first." How could she tell Lauren that Mary Ann wore a teal suit to the last New Year's Eve party they attended, two years ago?

Chapter Two

After another hour of unpacking, Lauren banished Maris to their bedroom while she changed clothes in the guest room. A provocative red dress with a plunging neckline had aroused Maris's attention, but Lauren preferred a tailored gray pin-striped suit. It was a stalemate when she left to try on a third selection.

Earnhardt, nervous and excited, ran from one end of the house to the other, following Lauren and racing down the hallway back to Maris. "I think it's warm enough for you to go outside and chase squirrels," she said. He danced behind her nosing the back of her legs until she opened the door.

Running to the bedroom, Maris dove on the bed and propped herself against the headboard with a pillow. Lauren appeared in the doorway wearing tight black pants and a matching blazer with a floral pattern over a white shell. Her green eyes gleamed seductively as she tossed her red hair. "Well?" she asked.

With her hands clasped behind her head, Maris grinned. "I like this one. Come here."

Lauren came to the side of the bed and leaned over to kiss her. "Is this okay for the party?" she asked. Maris grabbed her and pulled her onto the bed. She struggled briefly before jerking her arms free to brace herself. Smiling, she asked, "Now what?"

Maris twisted a strand of dangling red hair and ran her fingertips down Lauren's check. She gripped her behind the neck and drew her closer for a long kiss. "We better take these off now — you don't want to wear them out before the party."

Lauren sat upright, straddling Maris, and wiggled out of the blazer. Maris stretched to help with the white shell, but Lauren swept her hands away, hastily whipped off the shell and unsnapped her bra. Maris brushed the tips of her fingers across Lauren's aroused nipples before encircling her waist and caressing her back. They kissed. She flipped Lauren onto the bed beside her and, sliding both hands under the elastic bands of her pants and panties, stripped them off.

"No fair, you're still dressed," Lauren said, running her hand through Maris's hair.

Maris fumbled with the first button on her shirt until Lauren impatiently took over. She relaxed and fell back on the bed, allowing Lauren to unfasten her shirt and jeans and help her out of them. Her bra and panties soon followed. She nudged Lauren's shoulder, urging her to roll over.

"Not this time," Lauren said, resisting the pressure. Although she was stronger, Maris acquiesced. The scar on her right cheek tingled when Lauren traced it with a long red fingernail. While they were kissing, Maris shifted her upper body slightly and worked her hand between Lauren's legs. Her silken hair was damp where she parted the opening and found the warmth inside. She stroked gently until Lauren groaned in pleasure. She suppressed a shiver when Lauren grabbed the headboard and hoisted herself within reach of her lips. She greeted her eagerly. Soon Lauren stiffened and cried out.

Panting from exertion, Lauren weakly unwound her long legs and collapsed next to Maris. "God, Maris, is it possible to have a heart attack at thirty?" Maris laughed and nuzzled her neck. She waited in anticipation until Lauren recovered and, after a series of teasing caresses, settled between her thighs. When it was over, she felt like she'd strained every muscle. They lay quietly until Lauren struggled to the side of the bed. "I'll be right back, if I can walk."

When she returned, she handed Maris a damp cloth and a beer. "Would you believe we've been in here for nearly two hours?"

"No wonder I'm starving." Propping herself up against the headboard, she opened her beer and said, "I love you."

"I love you, too." Lauren crawled under the comforter. "Aren't you cold?"

"No, I feel lots of things right now, but cold ain't one of 'em. You're playing hell with my work schedule, and I haven't lifted weights since you came back from Chicago." Maris drank from her beer can.

"Don't worry you're getting plenty of exercise. You can return to your routine after New Year's."

"Speaking of New Year's, I'd like to drive to Austin Monday afternoon. That'll give us all of New Year's Eve in town."

"We can leave as soon as I get off work."

Slamming down the rest of her beer, Maris said, "I have something to show you." After putting on a pair of sweats and a T-shirt, she unlocked the lab and retrieved the box and the copy of the note. Wearing a maroon robe, Lauren met her in the den.

Maris turned on the halogen pole lamp. "Don't touch the shoe with your bare hands."

As she opened the box, Lauren said, "Honey, bring me a glass of wine instead of a — oh my, Lovelady shoes. Jesus, I haven't thought of them in years."

Maris poured Lauren a glass of zinfandel from a bottle in the refrigerator and grabbed a beer. "I got it and the note today. You know the brand?"

"Yes, Lovelady's department store in Austin carried them. I guess they had them specially manufactured. I don't know. Are you familiar with Lovelady's?"

"No, I don't shop much."

"No kidding!" Lauren laughed. "Well, Lovelady's went out of business in about 'eighty or 'eighty-one. My grandmother was devastated when they closed. She bought the shoes for my first dance there. I was thirteen, I think, and I still have them. The store was run by Heloise Lovelady. Rumors were that she was the mistress of a popular governor in the Forties. He bought her the store in downtown Austin to give her a legitimate reason to stay close to the Governor's mansion. They say many important political liaisons went on in her back office. What do you think this note means?"

"I'm not sure, but someone jacked off in the shoe."

"Disgusting! You fingerprinted it?"

"The shoe and the box. I don't want to fingerprint the note until I can get Shannon Stockwell to enhance the indentations. The shoe was clean of prints."

"Do you think this is a sick joke?"

"Maybe, but only information about the missing hand was leaked to the press. I can't imagine any of the guys carrying a joke this far."

"It's not Theresa Eastin's shoe?"

"No."

"Maybe the murderer sent it."

"Why would he? We have no leads on him at this time. This may give us one. I'm hoping we can trace the box using the UPS bar code on the shipping label. If it becomes important, I can run DNA on the sample from Theresa Eastin's body and the sperm from the shoe to determine if they're from the same man. But I'd rather not until we get a suspect."

"Tracing the UPS package is no problem. I can go

to their Web site on the Internet and check that."
Lauren frowned thoughtfully. "You were on the news
in your coveralls with *Middleton Forensic Services* on
the back. All he'd have to do is look in the phone
book for an address. Maybe he knows you'll be doing
the analysis in this case and is warning you off.
Everyone has heard of DNA these days. Suppose he's
afraid you'll link him to other murders. Or maybe
the reverse is true and there are other murders that
he wants you to know about. Maybe it's a challenge."

"You know this can't be his first crime." She sat
down on the sofa next to Lauren. "He has to know
that if I don't do the tests someone else will. Why
take a chance by sending us potential evidence? If
there are similar murders somewhere, we'd find out
eventually. Wayne should get a hit from Quantico
when he sends in the Violent Crime report."

"It takes a while to process the VICAP reports.
Do you think the age of the shoes is significant? I
know these shoes are at least sixteen years old."

"I don't know. They could have bought it at a
garage sale or Goodwill."

"To be safe, you have to seriously consider the
killer as the source of the note and shoe . . . even if
the age is odd. Have you told Wayne Coffey about
this?"

"I tried to call him today. But I forgot that he,
Ralph Lambert and ol' Sheriff Jake are hunting
mountain lions in Colorado. They won't be back to
work until the second or third." Maris frowned.
"Lauren, I vaguely remember hearing about a similar
murder when I was in training at the Austin DPS
lab. I can't remember any details, but I know a

retired chemist who'll remember if anything like this has happened in Texas before."

"Whether the man who sent this to you is involved in the murder or not, this could be a dangerous game. Whoever sent this knows where you live, where we live."

She looked genuinely worried and it touched Maris. She kissed her.

Chapter Three

Shortly after eight o'clock on Monday, the
thirtieth, Maris backed her 1970 red Oldsmobile 442
convertible out of the garage. She and Lauren had
spent all day Sunday unpacking and she was ready to
get out of the house for a while. Shannon was
expecting her and she caught herself looking forward
to the meeting. It was a beautiful day for a drive,
although it was not quite warm enough to put the
top down and Earnhardt seemed disappointed. He
curled up in the passenger seat and was asleep before
she reached the highway. The end of December had

been unseasonably warm with highs in the upper seventies and lows in the fifties. On her way back, she'd drop him off at Kathy and Lynn's with his favorite tennis ball and enough Iams to last until she returned. They'd agreed to baby-sit him, although it meant two nights and two days of living hell for Cricket, Kathy's Siamese cat.

Her thoughts returned to Shannon. She'd met the pretty blond, blue-eyed Fort Worth native at the Forensic Science Academy meeting in San Antonio in February of '94. They stumbled into each other at the ice breaker the first night and soon realized that they shared many of the same interests, including women, horses, the Dallas Cowboys and baseball. Shannon raised, trained and showed cutting horses and was a highly ranked amateur. Many thought she should go pro. As soon as feasible, they slipped away from their co-workers and raced to a gay bar near downtown San Antonio. She'd been excited to have a running buddy for the week. Unfortunately, neither Mary Ann nor Shannon's lover, Robin, were overjoyed at the situation and their enthusiasm for the new friendship deteriorated rapidly when Maris decided to move in with Shannon for the last three nights of the convention. The rooms in the Marriot River Center were expensive and the state spending allowance was not enough to pay for a place to stay and also cover part of the meals unless four employees roomed together. Despite her better judgment, Maris had agreed to share a room and two double beds with three straight women, including one who was pregnant. Two of the ladies paired off quickly, leaving Maris with the expectant mother, who chose the floor over sharing a bed with her. Maris couldn't decide if she was relieved or insulted, but it offended her sense of proper butch chivalry to allow a pregnant woman to sleep on the floor.

She thought the guardian angel for misplaced dykes was looking out for her when Shannon's roommate, who had already paid her bill, was forced to cancel at the last minute due to a court scheduling conflict. Shannon didn't have to ask her more than once to change rooms.

The arrangement was innocent, but the lovers at home remained less than secure. Shortly after noon on Thursday, the hotel staff handed Shannon a message that someone was in the lobby to see her. It was Robin, who decided to take the rest of the week off to visit San Antonio. Maris teased Shannon unmercifully the rest of the day. Payback came at four-thirty when they returned to the room and found Mary Ann and Robin happily sharing a bottle of expensive wine, charged to Shannon. In fact, they looked so comfortable that it crossed Maris's mind that maybe the wrong half of the foursome had been worried. Mary Ann swore to Maris that she'd planned to surprise her in San Antonio all along and only moved her reservation up one day. So Maris changed rooms for the second time. Later she figured out that it had cost her and Mary Ann about seven hundred dollars for the pregnant lady to have her own bed.

Maris parked the Olds directly in front of Shannon's office on the corner of Jones Street and East Belknap in downtown Fort Worth. It was a short walking distance from her office to the old Criminal Justice Court, the old civil courthouse, the Fort Worth Police Department and the new Justice Center next to the Tandy Center shopping and business complex. Shannon's building, made of handsome red brick, was very old and there'd been talk of registering it as a historical landmark. Carrying the envelope with the note, she pushed open the heavy wooden door and greeted Timothy, Shannon's receptionist. He called Shannon on the intercom and came around the desk to hug Maris and pat Earnhardt.

Shannon, wearing an unbuttoned blue lab coat over a belted navy skirt and a white ribbed sweater, hugged Maris and stooped to talk to Earnhardt who promptly licked her on the cheek. Standing, she said, "First things first. Tell us about Lauren."

"Yes, girl," Timothy said, returning to his desk. "Tell all."

"Lie down, fellow." Maris tossed Earnhardt a raw- hide bone she pulled from her hip pocket. He grabbed the bone and flopped down in the corner near Timothy's desk. Grinning, she shrugged. "What's to tell? She's good-looking, redheaded. A great dancer. Has a good sense of humor —"

"Obviously, if she's moving in with you." Shannon laughed.

"Thanks a lot." Studying Shannon, Maris noticed for the first time her pale complexion and the dark circles under her blue eyes. "You remember Sherf?"

"Do I?" Shannon rolled her eyes. "What a character."

Sherf, one of the first female sheriffs in Texas, had served a county in the High Plains for over forty years, and Maris admired her a lot. She said, "I stayed with her for a week when I was out there to testify on a clandestine speed lab we'd busted. There was a red-headed juror that Sherf was infatuated

23

with. She told me strawberry roans and red-headed women were more dangerous than the Texas weather, but everyone ought to have one of each at least once in their lifetime. Twice if you were tough enough."

"At least I've had the strawberry roan." Shannon winked at Timothy. "Threw me into a fence post and broke two of my ribs."

"You're encouraging," Maris said, frowning playfully.

Timothy asked, "Is she really FBI?"

"Yes, I'll have to bring her over someday." Watching Shannon's eyes, Maris said, "I'm looking forward to introducing her to you and Robin."

"I'm looking forward to meeting her. I don't know if Robin . . . will . . . be available." Shannon's smile faded. Maris caught Timothy's glance. He grimaced. Shannon took Maris's hand. "Come into the lab. Let me finish with the will I'm looking at and then we'll start with your case."

The tiredness in Shannon's voice troubled Maris. When the lab door closed behind them, Maris put her arms around Shannon and hugged her. It was no secret that Robin fucked around. She'd even made an unsuccessful run on Mary Ann right after they returned from the San Antonio trip. After making Maris promise not to get angry, Mary Ann told her that Robin had called and asked her out for a drink — alone. She had refused. Despite the promise, Maris wanted to drive to Fort Worth and clip Robin's wings, but Mary Ann held her to her word. She never told Shannon. Last June, Maris met Kathy and Lynn at Friends, a lesbian bar in Dallas, to spend a rainy Saturday afternoon shooting pool. Inadvertently, she surprised Robin in a corner booth wrapped around a tall brunette. Robin made awkward introductions and soon left with the brunette in tow. The next time she talked to Shannon, she mentioned running into Robin. After a long silence, Shannon had replied, "It's okay, Maris. I know she's cheating and it's not the first time. Let's just leave it at that."

Shannon felt small and fragile, but Maris knew her size was deceiving. After years of working horses and hauling hay and feed, she was stronger than expected. Her voice was muffled against Maris's chest when she asked, "Is it that obvious?"

"You look beautiful as ever — but tired. Do you want to talk about it?"

She pushed away from Maris. "It's the same thing over and over. She swears she loves me and doesn't want anyone else. She refuses to move out of the house, but every few months there's another woman, another affair. They don't last very long and she's always sorry afterwards. This time it's some kid from TCU that she met at the bar."

"Why do you stay with her?"

"I'm finally beginning to ask myself that same question." She laughed, but to Maris it seemed forced. "We've been in counseling for six months. I thought it was helping until I found out about her latest." She blinked back tears. "I guess I still love her."

Maris stared at the floor, swallowing her words. How could anyone continuously hurt a woman like Shannon?

"It's been a hard week. You know Buster?"

"Yes, I remember him." Maris knew Buster was a quarter horse gelding Shannon had owned since she was thirteen.

"He's twenty-two years old. I haven't used him in competition in ages, but he's still my favorite. He hasn't been doing well lately and I'm worried. I'm afraid the vet will tell me it's time to put him down. I don't need this, especially now."

"Is there anything I can do?"

Shannon twisted a ring on her hand. "I don't know."

"If you need help with him, all you have to do is call me."

"I appreciate it, but I'm afraid when the time comes we may not have much warning."

"That's okay. I'll work it out."

Shannon paced a few steps away and turned to face her, crossing her arms. "My meeting you has been hard on Robin. She resents you. She says that I want her to be like you."

It'd have been a lot harder on her, Maris thought, if Mary Ann hadn't stepped in to save her sorry hide. "Maybe it wouldn't hurt her to be a little more like me. If we were together, I'd never cheat on you." As soon as she said it, she regretted it.

"I know, and you won't cheat on Lauren either."

"No," Maris said, frowning at the toe of her boot.

When she looked up, the tears were drying in Shannon's blue eyes, and they were beginning to twinkle mischievously. Leaning on the counter next to her microscope, she said, "I find myself wishing I'd thrown Robin out back in the summer."

"I wasn't ready for another relationship then."

Looking up, Maris grinned. "Besides it might ruin a good friendship."

"Well, someday, if the timing is right for both of us, I might be willing to risk it." Before Maris could answer, Shannon turned and bent over a microscope. Looking through the eyepieces, she turned the focus knob and studied a signature on someone's last will and testament. Attaching a camera to one of the oculars, she snapped a couple of pictures. Removing the document and the camera, she said, "Okay, that's it for this case. Tell me about yours."

Maris brought her up to date on the Theresa Eastin murder investigation, describing the mutilation of the body in detail. She showed her a photograph of the black Lovelady shoe that accompanied the warning note.

"Lovelady shoes. Lord, I haven't thought of them in years. My mother and older sisters spent a fortune in that store. My dad flew them to Austin twice a year to buy shoes. Anyone who was anyone in Texas back then wore Lovelady heels."

Although Shannon rarely mentioned it, Maris knew her family was wealthy. *Texas Monthly* once ran an in-depth article about her father. He had worked for the Bass brothers before starting his own wildcat drilling company and earning his first few million in West Texas crude oil. Smart enough to diversify into other industries, he sheltered the bulk of his wealth from the ups and downs of the oil business. The bust in the Eighties barely phased him. He was a player in Texas politics and close to former President Bush and his son, George W., the Texas governor. Somehow the article failed to mention how the great Texan disowned his beautiful and intelligent youngest daughter for the unforgivable sin of loving another woman and forbade her mother and siblings from seeing or talking to her. Shannon hadn't stepped foot in her family mansion since she was a senior in college. Generously — although that seemed a dubious description to Maris — he left Shannon's trust fund intact. So at least she could indulge her passion for horses, although Maris wondered how much Shannon really depended on the money. After a six-year apprenticeship as a questioned documents examiner for the Tarrant County Sheriff's office, she'd opened her own lab and was considered one of the best independent examiners in the country.

Shannon donned a pair of latex gloves and carefully removed the note from the envelope. Placing it on a white examining board surrounded by four powerful lights, she examined it through a magnifying lens. Shannon read out loud. " 'I KNOW WHO AND WHAT YOU ARE. STAY AWAY.' Do you think he knows you're gay?"

"I don't know. Lauren thinks he knows I'm a forensic chemist and is warning me to stay out of the investigation. Maybe, with all of the publicity about DNA, he's afraid I can put him away. Doesn't make much sense to me. DNA is worthless until the police develop a suspect — at least for now. Someday, when the CODIS program is off of the ground and the DNA database of known sex offenders is on-line, we may be able to develop a suspect from body fluids left after the assault — if he's a repeat sex offender and in our database."

"Well, you're in luck on your note here. There's no writing on the back of the page to interfere and it looks like your guy is heavy-handed with his pen. Some of the marks are overlapping, but we'll be able to read a few of them." Moving the document to a table with an overhead Polaroid camera, Shannon turned on a bright spotlight and lowered it, forming a sharp oblique angle to the surface of the paper. After studying several lens filters, she chose one, attached it to the camera and took a photograph. After the Polaroid film developed, she handed the picture to Maris.

"Not bad," Shannon said, looking over her shoulder. "Looks like several phone numbers and some writing is visible. He bears down hard enough on his pen that I think we're seeing impressions from the top two or three sheets. Looks like a doodle page of some sort. Maybe a telephone scratch pad?"

"No, it's a computer scratch pad. Some of this looks like e-mail and Internet addresses."

"I'm going to change to the thirty-five millimeter camera and take more pictures under the oblique lighting. We'll try a couple of other filters. When I develop the film I'll enlarge the photographs." She had her own darkroom. "Afterwards, we'll try another technique. I might be able to raise some more of the indentations using ESDA — the Electrostatic Detection Apparatus."

"I've read about it in the *Journal of Forensic Science.*"

"It's usually more efficient than photographic techniques, especially on papers with indentations on one side and other writings on the back. I can digitally enhance the readability of the ESDA lifts, but I don't think it'll be necessary on this. It's pretty clean."

After Shannon completed the photography, Maris followed her to the other side of the room. Shannon worked quickly as she talked.

"The ESDA is a non-destructive technique. I'll cover the document with a polymer film, put an electrical charge on it and spray it with electrostatic copier toner to develop an image of the indented strokes. I can then preserve the image by covering it with a transparent adhesive plastic sheet or by photographing it. Since you want to look for fingerprints later, we'll use photography. The writings will appear black on a gray background on the ESDA print. When I'm finished, you can take the note back if you want to take a chance that my pictures will come out okay. I'll blow the ESDA print up to scale using high contrast black and white film."

"Okay, I'm supposed to be in Fort Worth for court on Thursday. I'll call you. Maybe I can get the pictures then."

It was almost noon when Shannon handed the envelope with the yellow sheet of paper to Maris. "I need to check on Buster. Why don't you go with me? You can buy my lunch at Joe T. Garcia's and then we'll drive out there."

"I don't know. I have Earnhardt with me and I need to —"

"Oh, come on. Earnhardt can go with us. It's cool enough for him to wait in the car while we eat."

"Okay, you twisted my arm." Sorry, Earnhardt, she thought, a beautiful blond and Mexican food beats a Quarter Pounder with you any day.

* * * * *

Maris was ready and waiting at three-thirty when Lauren arrived home from work. Anxious not to waste time, she called Edward Evers, a retired trace- evidence expert, and arranged to drop by his home in Georgetown on their way to Austin. Despite Lauren's reservations about the unpredictable Texas weather, Maris insisted they take the convertible. By seven o'clock, they were ringing Edward's door bell. He answered quickly and invited them into a spacious, decidedly masculine den decorated with antique six- shooters and other western paraphernalia. He was a clean-shaven man of seventy with sparkling gray eyes. Slightly stooped, he was over six feet tall with large smooth hands that engulfed Maris's when he greeted her. As her mentor, he'd taught her the finer points of hair, fiber and paint analysis. Although he retired from DPS at sixty-five, he was not one to remain idle and taught chemistry classes at Austin College before launching a new career as a mystery writer.

When Maris introduced him to Lauren, his eyes lit up and he eagerly pumped her for information about the FBI while he poured her a glass of white wine. Since his den seemed to call for whiskey, Maris requested Jack Daniel's on ice. He gave them their drinks before preparing scotch and water for himself. The polite conversation lagged when he sat down in a large leather chair across the coffee table from them. He asked, "What brings you here, Maris? I know it's not just to see an old man."

Maris felt the Tennessee sipping whiskey warming her chest. She cleared her throat and told him about the Theresa Eastin case and the threat she had received along with the black heel. Pulling three photographs from her jacket pocket, she handed them across the table to Edward.

He set his drink down and reached for the pictures. He stared silently at the first one. Shaking his head sadly, he glanced at the others and said, "God, I'd hoped never to see another murder like this again, even in photographs." He took a long sip of his scotch and water. "I've seen similar mutilations twice before and each time one of the victim's shoes were missing. You say you received a shoe in the mail?"

"By UPS, but it's not like the victim's remaining shoe."

"It's a Lovelady shoe," Lauren said.

Edward fumbled with his drink, almost dropping it. He picked up the photograph Maris tossed on the table of the black stiletto-heeled shoe and stared at it. "It's not possible. Not after all of these years." He looked up. "There were two murders like this in Austin. The first girl was found near Lake Travis off highway fourteen thirty-one close to Bee Caves Road in March of 'eighty. The second body was discovered a month later — almost to the day — near the same place. Both women — I still remember their names, Debbie Keisler and Cynthia Allen — wore black Lovelady shoes, but they were slightly different in style. One could be like this. I don't know; it's been so long." He threw down the last of his drink and went to the bar to fix a second. "It's preposterous to think this is the Allen or Keisler shoe. Hell, it's preposterous to think the Pierce county murder is related after seventeen years. But what are the odds of another murderer using the same bizarre methodology?"

"It could be a coincidence. Two sick minds that think alike. Or it could be a copycat who's read about the 'eighty murders," Maris said.

He dropped back in his chair and stared at a painting over her head. After a moment, he said, "None of the information about the amputation of the left hand or missing shoe was released to the press. Later we were all placed under a gag order. The only suspect was the son of a state senator from Houston. We had no real proof against him. He was a dope fiend, worked as a stock boy and janitor at Lovelady's department store. Had a couple of priors for burglary and a peeping tom arrest. The senator couldn't have stopped us if we'd had something solid, but the investigation languished for lack of evidence, new leads. We had good people, our best, working on this case. Albert Wheeler was the Austin detective in charge. The Texas Rangers were called in to assist. We never gave up." He sipped his drink and frowned. "Albert called me about two years ago. He's retired but said he had a new lead. He said he'd let me know if anything came of it, but I never heard from him."

"Who was conducting the investigation for the lab?"

"I was in charge. Bill Rogers, the DPS photographer, and Barbara Shelton, the serologist, went to both scenes. The missing shoes and hands were never found. At first, we thought that he went for women with a wedding ring or engagement ring on her hand. Thus, the symbolism of the missing left hand, but Cynthia Allen wasn't married or engaged. Both women wore red fingernail polish. When we realized they had the same brand of black heels,

Lovelady's, we keyed on Hatcher." He took a deep breath.

"What is it, Edward?"

"I'm an old man, Maris. I've seen a lot of horrible things in my life but these two murders were among the worst."

"What kind of physical evidence did you have?"

"We had nothing. Barbara did the serological testing on the case. No semen or foreign blood was found on either of the bodies. Fibers were nondescript. A shoeprint was found next to one of them, but it was accidentally destroyed before we could get a cast or even a decent photograph. The most intriguing and promising piece of evidence was a partial fingernail found in Cynthia Allen's hair. But William Roy had extremely short nails when he was brought in for questioning. No torn ones. He let Albert Wheeler search his apartment and no shoes were found that could have left the print we saw at the scene. No bloody clothes were found. Nothing to tie him to the women or to the murders, except that he worked at Lovelady's."

"These days the broken fingernail could be analyzed using DNA and compared to known blood and a fingernail from William Roy. Why hasn't it been done?"

"I don't know. I would guess that there is no basis for a search warrant to force William Roy to give the blood. Maybe no one has thought of it. I hope DPS still has the fingernail, but who knows? Maybe it's lost."

"God, I hope not," Maris said. "As sensational as these cases were, why didn't I hear more about them when I was in training at the Austin lab?"

34

"Well, most of the details were kept from the general public, and I would've been the only one left in the lab who saw the bodies. This case wasn't exactly a stellar success. You notice we only use the good ones in training." He swirled the ice in his glass. "These cases have haunted a lot of people. Barbara quit only six months after the murders. She was one of the first women hired by the lab and had a Ph.D. in biochemistry with an emphasis in genetics. I think DPS would have had a DNA program much sooner if she'd stayed. Bill Rogers had nightmares for months and Albert Wheeler was obsessed with solving the murders to the point that it hurt his other cases. Maybe you should call him."

He gave them Wheeler's phone number. She and Lauren thanked him for the drink and the information. Edward poured himself a third drink before escorting them to the door. Maris thought he seemed somewhat older and much sadder than when they arrived.

Chapter Four

The last morning of the year was warm with clear blue skies. Maris squinted in the bright light that filtered into the lobby of the Austin Police Department and wondered, as she waited for Albert Wheeler's son, why sons and daughters follow their fathers into police work. You would think they, of all people, should know better. But she hadn't and apparently neither did Albert Wheeler's son.

She yawned and Lauren punched her in the arm. "Stop that. You'll have me doing it."

After leaving Edward's house, they had checked

into their hotel room in downtown Austin and met Amy and Maris's sister, Lana, for a late meal. They were late getting to bed, but Maris was up early making the phone calls that led to the meeting with the Austin detective.

When a heavyset officer in plainclothes approached and introduced himself as Albert Wheeler, Jr., Maris shifted the paper sack with the Lovelady black heel to her other hand and grasped his beefy right hand. "Please call me Al," he said, when Maris introduced him to Lauren.

"I'm sorry about your father," Lauren said.

"Thanks. Alzheimer's is a terrible disease. He's completely bedridden now."

"It was nice of your mother to put us in touch with you. How long have you been a detective?" Maris asked.

"Three years. My father knew I got my detective shield. I'm grateful for that." He smiled, stroking the thick brown mustache that swept just past the corners of his mouth. "A friend asked me if I knew anything about a body that was found with a hand missing. I never saw anything in the paper or the news and forgot about it until you called this morning."

Maris said, "Only one TV news report mentioned the hand was missing, and they didn't let out any other information. The Texas Ranger investigating the case, Wayne Coffey, tried to keep the details out of the media."

"My father and the other investigators did the same thing in 'eighty. You said that Edward told you about William Roy and the gag order?"

Maris nodded. Carrying two thick manila folders,

he led them to a windowless conference room near the Austin laboratory. "Even if the shoe you received is a sick joke, it has to be from someone with inside knowledge about the Keisler and Allen murders. But I don't see how they could possibly know the brand."

An evidence technician, a pretty brunette, pushed a squeaking stainless steel cart bearing four dusty brown file boxes covered in faded initials, case numbers and dates almost two decades old. The clear tape originally used to seal the evidence was brittle and yellow and broke easily when she pulled the flaps to open the boxes.

"This is Lynn Stephens, our evidence tech," Al said. "She'll stay in here with the evidence while we examine it. Technically, it'll still be in her possession."

Maris nodded, thinking that Lynn must have been in elementary school when the murders occurred. At least Maris had been a sophomore in high school.

Lynn smiled shyly. "I'll put the evidence from each murder on opposite ends of the table so we can open them both without getting any of it mixed up. I also brought a box of gloves." She tossed a box of blue nitrile gloves onto the table. Maris slipped on a pair and waited while Lynn carried one of the boxes to the opposite end of the table and took several brown paper sacks from it. She carefully slit the tops of the bags containing the evidence from Cynthia Allen's murder and arranged the soiled, ragged clothing, a single left shoe, a white sexual assault evidence collection kit and a purse on one end of the table. Maris picked up the torn clothing. Seventeen years later it was the same as when the laboratory completed their analysis and resealed the evidence.

Dirt and dried grass clung to the beige blouse and ripped navy skirt. Dark crusted blood stained the front of the blouse and there was a faint odor of death. She studied the knot on the pantyhose, noticing the sharp cut where someone released them from her neck. Setting Cynthia's black Lovelady shoe in front of her, she opened the sack she brought with her. The shoes were different styles. She caught Lauren's eyes and shrugged, feeling foolish in her disappointment.

Turning her attention to Debbie Keisler's evidence, Maris cursorily looked at her stained dress and pantyhose. Impatiently, she watched as Lynn slit the last paper sack and a black shoe with a three-inch heel fell on the table.

"Goddamn," Al said as Maris held the right shoe side by side with the Keisler left shoe.

"Could it really be hers?" Lauren asked.

Maris looked inside each shoe comparing them. Flipping the shoes over she perused the soles and heels. "The size is the same, the style is the same, and each shoe has about the same amount of wear on the sole." A chill ran through her as she set the shoes on the table and dropped into a chair. "I really thought it was a joke — or coincidence."

"My father never stopped working on these cases, even after he retired. Jesus, why now? Why surface now?"

"Maybe he just got out of jail for something else," Maris said. "Or maybe he's been active all along in another state or country."

"Wouldn't we have heard about it?" Lauren asked.

"Well, it's a new ballgame now," Maris said, returning to the Allen evidence. She reached for the sexual assault kit and broke the seal. Quickly, she inventoried the items inside. "I don't see the fingernail here anywhere."

"I think the DPS lab retained it," Al said.

She handed the kit to Lynn and opened the case folders. Lauren came around the table and sat next to her. Maris spread the crime scene photos across the table. "Lord, it's like Edward said. The bodies are positioned like Theresa Eastin's was. The genital mutilation is similar. Theresa Eastin's pantyhose were tied around her neck the same way. It has to be the same killer." Cynthia's purse caught her eye and, partially rising from her chair, she grabbed it. Pushing the file folders away, she unsnapped the silver fastener. "Why do you still have Cynthia's purse?"

Al walked around the table and stood behind her, leaning over her shoulder. "Usually, if none of the personal items seem to have a bearing on the case, we inventory them and return them to the family. I guess we kept it because no one came forward to claim it."

Maris started to dump the contents of the purse on the table and paused. It seemed disrespectful so she lifted the items out of the purse a handful at a time, gently setting them down. She never carried a purse and it felt odd to open a stranger's.

Lauren leaned against her, watching as she turned the pages of Cynthia's address book. Except for the names listed under "school," the others were all female. Lauren caught a page as Maris flipped it and pointed to the name, Barbara Shelton, and a telephone number. She wrote it down while Maris kept reading.

"I know this woman," Maris said, stopping at another name. She handed the address book to Lauren who wrote down the second name and number. "In fact, she sometimes attends Amy's parties. We might see her tonight." Maris sorted through the remaining items in the purse — a movie ticket stub from *A Star Is Born*, a tube of lipstick, a compact, and a wallet with a checkbook and fifteen dollars in cash. A small amount of change was in the bottom of the purse. She absently smoothed the wrinkled receipts for groceries, a dress from J.C. Penney, and dry cleaning. Turning over the last piece of paper, she said, "This is a speeding ticket from Austin P.D. issued two days before she was killed." She handed it to Lauren.

Lauren asked, "Al, can we get photocopies of all of these receipts, the ticket and the address book?"

"Hell, why not, since you're FBI. I assume we'll reopen these investigations now anyway."

He left to make the copies while Lauren studied the official investigation and autopsy reports, occasionally jotting down notes. Maris looked through the remaining evidence and dwelled over the photographs, unsuccessfully searching for a picture of the shoeprint Edward said was destroyed at the scene. When they were finished, Lynn methodically returned each item to its original container, taped it, initialed and dated the seal.

As they prepared to leave, Maris thanked Al for his help. "When Wayne and the boys get back into town, I'll let them know what we've found out so far. I imagine he'll contact you."

"Proving William Roy Hatcher was guilty was my father's obsession. I'd like to help nail him, especially if he's started back killing."

"Do you know where he is now?" Lauren asked.

"No, I've heard he's been in and out of drug rehab and mental institutions for years, but I don't know where. Supposedly, he's mildly schizophrenic and requires medication."

"Your father told Edward Evers about two years ago that he had a new lead. Do you know what he was working on?"

"He had volumes of spiral notebooks with information on the murders. I've been meaning to read them but haven't. I'll go through them tomorrow while I watch the Cotton Bowl and Rose Bowl games. If I find anything to help you, I'll let you know. I don't expect to find much. He had symptoms of Alzheimer's long before it finally incapacitated him."

Silently, they left the police station. Although a cloud bank was visible to the north, the sun was bright and warm and Maris lowered the white convertible top.

"Maris," Lauren said, putting a slender hand on her arm. "Cynthia Allen was a lesbian."

"I'm not sure we can infer that from her address book."

"Most of the numbers listed belonged to women. Isn't it odd she had Barbara Shelton's number? What if they were lovers, or ex-lovers?"

"Don't speculate — we don't know how well they knew each other, assuming they did. It might even be another Barbara Shelton."

"At the very least, I think they were friends. It could explain why the murders haunted Barbara and why she quit DPS soon afterwards. I think it's worth exploring. Besides, she was a teacher and Barbara was one of the first women hired by the lab. If they were lesbians, they'd have been discreet. What about your friend she had listed in her address book?"

"Diane Cooper?" Maris laughed. "Half of the women in Austin can confirm that Diane's a lesbian. If she's at the party, I'll ask her about Cynthia Allen. As long as we're in Austin, let's drop by the DPS building for a visit. They probably have a current phone number for Barbara."

The December sun felt good to Maris, but the rapidly approaching black line of clouds from the north threatened a change. This case was already bizarre, with a murderer apparently reappearing after seventeen years. Was it possible that Barbara Shelton had investigated the rape-murder of her friend? God, what if they *were* lovers or ex-lovers? Deep in thought, as they drove down Lamar toward the DPS headquarters building, Maris almost rear-ended a Chevrolet pickup when Lauren surprised her with a change in subject.

"Are you and Amy ex-lovers?" she asked.

"What makes you ask that?" And why at this particular place and time, she wanted to add.

"She seems to know you very well."

"She should. She's known me since college when we were eighteen or nineteen."

"So were you lovers?"

"Are you going to ask this question about everyone you meet down here?" Maris glanced at her.

"No, just her."

43

Turning into the front parking lot of the DPS headquarters on Lamar, Maris ignored Lauren and searched for a parking place. Cutting sharply into a visitor's space between two pickups, Maris felt Lauren watching her as she put the top up on the convertible before cutting the engine. She almost laughed, thinking about Lauren's question, but held back, knowing it would be a dead giveaway. Although her affair with Amy had been short, ending when the ice melted after a frigid three-day weekend, it had been intense, energetic and, goddamn, it had been fun. Whether it was their youth, the newness of the experience, the lack of inhibition since there was no threat of commitment, or simply isolation and boredom due to the weather, she didn't know. But it had been an extraordinary experience. They'd agreed not to tell any of their friends and Maris hadn't. And they'd never tried it again, as if sensing it couldn't be the same. But it added a poignancy to their friendship, strengthening the affection they had for each other.

As they walked up the sidewalk, Lauren asked, "Well?"

"Well, what?"

"I see you smiling, Maris Mantle Middleton. Are you going to answer my question?"

She laughed, throwing open the glass door to the lobby. A gray-headed receptionist behind a chest-high counter rose and smiled. "We were beginning to think you'd never come back to visit us, Maris."

"Betty, it's good to see you. This is Lauren O'Conner, FBI. We're combining business with pleasure this trip checking on some old cases. By the way, do you remember Barbara Shelton?"

Betty nodded as she showed them where to sign the visitor's admittance register. "Yes, of course, I remember her. She was our first female chemist. Caused quite a stir when she was hired, but she handled herself well and showed the boys a thing or two."

"Do you know where she is now?"

"She went to work for IBM for a while and I lost touch with her. I missed her when she quit."

"Thanks, Betty, it was good to see you again," Maris said as the elevator doors opened.

They rode to the second floor and entered a small lobby with a receptionist's desk. Several seats lined the wall under a large picture window that looked out on Lamar and part of the parking lot. A set of double doors in the back of the lobby led to the laboratory where analytical services in drug analysis, toxicology, serology, DNA, questioned document examinations, firearms, forensic photography and latent fingerprints were performed.

Maris didn't recognize the second-floor receptionist. She asked for Bob Stocklin and within minutes he was in the lobby pumping her hand. She introduced him to Lauren and, true to form, he immediately began to flirt. A handsome man, graying at the temples as he approached fifty, he had only recently left the bench for a desk job as lab manager.

"We came to ask you about the nineteen eighty murders of two women, Debbie Keisler and Cynthia Allen." Briefly, she told him about the recent murder in Pierce.

"I can't tell you much," he said. "Hell, we don't even have a hard copy of the files anymore. They've been microfilmed." He shoved his hands into his pockets and rattled his change. "I hadn't been here long and didn't work on those murders, but the whole lab followed the cases. I think frustration over the lack of progress cost us two good people, Barbara Shelton and Bill Rogers. We were ordered not to release information to anyone except the Ranger assigned to the case and the lead Austin P.D. detective. The Ranger is dead — killed in an attempt to stop a kidnapper — and the Austin detective is retired."

"I don't want you to go out on a limb. Wayne will be back soon and can arrange to get the records then. I'd appreciate it if you could give me Barbara Shelton's phone number and address . . . and also one for Bill Rogers, if you have it. A key piece of evidence in the Cynthia Allen case was a fingernail found in her hair. Austin P.D. doesn't have it. Wayne will want to know if you do."

"We'll pull the files off microfilm and have them ready for him. I'll check on any evidence that we may have and let him know when he calls." He returned to his office to find the numbers.

Maris smiled as a tall secretary came into the lobby, "Hello, Jean. How's DPS surviving without me?"

"Boring, Maris, very boring. These new kids they're hiring don't know how to have fun, and they damned sure don't know how to work. Not like we did when we started."

"I don't know about the work part, but we had the fun down pretty good."

Despite being divorced three times before she turned forty, Jean somehow showed no signs of aging except for the lines etched around the corners of her eyes and her tight smile. And she was still pretty. She asked, "So why'd you wait so long to come see us?"

"Too busy, I work all the time now that I don't have a cushy state job." Maris grinned and lowered her voice. "Jean, you remember Bill Rogers in photography?"

"Yes, I was afraid you'd ask when I heard you talking about the murders."

"I've got a similar case. I understand he was the photographer."

"He was. I remember those murders. Bill said they were the worst he'd ever seen."

"Why did he leave DPS?"

"He took portraits for individuals part-time. A woman accused him of assaulting her during one of the sessions. Another woman came forward later with similar accusations. I don't think any criminal charges were filed. Last I heard he was working for a newspaper as a free-lance photographer."

Bob returned with a folded piece of paper. "It seems inconceivable that your murder and the nineteen eighty murders could be related, but we'll do what we can to help. Have Wayne Coffey contact us when he gets back."

"Thanks for the information. How about a quick lab tour for Lauren?"

"Now, that's an easy request to fill." He laughed and opened the hall door leading to the lab.

After the tour, they left the DPS building in a downpour and ran to the Oldsmobile. Maris shivered as she started the engine and turned on the defroster. "Damn, it turned cold quickly."

Lauren shook the water from her red hair. "Can

47

you imagine cold weather and rain this time of year." A large drop of water formed under the convertible canopy and dropped to the console between them. Maris glared at her and Lauren coyly flipped her hair back over her shoulder. She asked, "Where does Barbara Shelton live now?"

Maris unfolded the piece of paper with the address and said, "Benbrook, southwest of Fort Worth. Bill Rogers is in Houston." Shoving the paper into her pocket, Maris watched the wipers fight a losing battle against a wall of water. "There's something else that I've been thinking about. Cynthia Allen and Debbie Keisler were killed a month apart. Theresa Eastin disappeared on the Friday after Thanksgiving."

"I know what you're thinking. If he stayed on the same schedule, he should have taken another victim around Christmas."

"There's a lot we don't know. Doesn't do much to put you in a party mood, does it?"

"No, but I'm looking forward to meeting your friends. By the way, you never answered my question."

"No," Maris said, laughing as she backed the Oldsmobile out of the parking place.

"No, you're not ex-lovers, or no, you aren't going to answer me?"

"You figure it out; you're the FBI agent."

Chapter Five

Lauren collapsed on the king-size bed in the hotel room while Maris opened the curtains to look out at downtown Austin. It had stopped raining and the view of the state capital was spectacular. Small now, compared to the towering office buildings surrounding it, the white building, still decked out for the holidays, sparkled beautifully. Turning from the window, Maris opened the Coleman cooler and dug around in the ice for a beer.

"Bring me one, lover," Lauren said. "I'm dying for a shower or maybe a long, hot bath."

Maris handed her a beer and plopped down on the bed next to her, using the pillow as a backrest against the headboard. "We have plenty of time before we have to get ready."

"Good, a nap would be nice."

"You can't waste the last few hours of the year napping." She turned on the television with the remote, flipping through channels. "I'll bet we have a bowl game on this afternoon."

"You can't waste the last few hours of the year watching a football game," Lauren teased, kissing her on the cheek. "And I really could use a nap. But I think I'll take that long, hot bath instead."

Maris grinned as Lauren slid off of the bed. She sipped her beer until she heard the water running, then finished it in one long swallow before she jumped to her feet. After kicking off her boots, her fingers flew across the buttons on her blouse and the zipper on her jeans. Stripping them off, she tossed them onto the bed. Discarding her underwear on the floor, she took another beer out of the cooler and quietly walked to the partially opened bathroom door.

Lauren stood naked before the mirror and brushed her shoulder-length red hair. She twisted it into a knot and secured it with a rubber band. Leaning over the tub, she poured bubble bath into the water. A light floral fragrance filled the room as the bubbles formed. She lowered the lid on the commode and placed a razor, her beer and a wash-cloth on top. As she turned toward the tub, Maris sprang through the door, stepped over the side and dropped into the water. Startled, Lauren screamed and dropped the hotel soap.

"Goddamn, this water is hot," Maris said, leaning

over to put the unopened beer on their porcelain table.

"Serves you right if you burn your ass. You almost gave me a heart attack. I thought you were watching football."

"I decided to join you instead."

"You could have asked first. If you had given me a chance, I might have invited you." She retrieved the bar of soap and, standing with her hand cocked on her hip, added, "I've a good mind to leave you in here by yourself. How am I supposed to shave my legs with you in the way?"

"I'm sorry if I scared you," Maris said, flashing what she hoped was her cutest and best dimpled grin. "Get in. I'll help you shave your legs."

Lauren laughed, tossing the soap at Maris. "I'm not sure I want any help." She gingerly stepped into the water, putting a hand on each side as she lowered herself and sat cross-legged facing Maris.

Maris moved closer to her and rose slightly to reach for the razor. She kissed Lauren and stroked her thigh. "Straighten your leg," she said.

Lauren folded a towel four times before laying it across the faucet to form a backrest. She leaned against the towel and timidly stretched out her leg.

"Don't worry, darling. I'll be careful."

"I don't know about this. I've seen blood dripping after you've shaved your own legs."

"Have a little faith, sweetheart, you're supposed to trust your lover."

"Trust, what a novel idea," Lauren said, a smile playing on the corners of her lips.

Maris held Lauren's right leg across her knee and against her side. Beginning where her thigh rose from the bubbles, she worked the soapsuds into a lather all the way to her toes. Smoothly and deliberately, she started the razor on the top of Lauren's foot and worked partially up her shin. Pausing occasionally to rinse the blade, she soon finished the lower half and started around her knee. Leaning forward, she kissed her.

After a long, tender kiss, Lauren said huskily, "You never fail to surprise me."

Maris smiled, carefully shaving Lauren's upper thigh. Purposely, she allowed her hand to stray underwater and brush against the hair between her legs. When she finished with the first leg, Maris slid back to the end of the tub, rinsed off the soap and rubbed her hands across the smooth leg.

"See, no blood," Maris said, setting the razor aside and popping the top of her beer. She took a drink and set the can down. "Now, for the other one."

Without a word, Lauren extended her other leg. Using the same procedure, Maris carefully shaved it.

Lauren leaned toward her, almost dropping her backrest into the water, and kissed her. "I can't believe you did both legs without even a scratch."

"Anything else you want shaved, sweetheart?"

"Not in this lifetime," Lauren answered quickly before kissing her again.

Maris caressed Lauren's nipples and they began to swell beneath her touch. She pressed harder against Lauren's lips, opening them with her tongue. After a lingering kiss, she said, "The water's getting cold."

"I hadn't noticed."

"Turn around with your back against me. Let some water out and run in some hot."

Lauren finished the last of her beer while she ran in the hot water. Maris uncrossed her legs and pulled Lauren close to her. She kissed her bare shoulders, working up her neck to her ear.

"Don't you even think about it. Leave my ear alone." She twisted away, giggling. "You know I can't stand that."

Maris took the rubber band out of Lauren's hair and watched as the thick auburn curls cascaded to her shoulders. She wrapped her arms around Lauren's waist and nuzzled her hair. Lauren tossed her head baring her shoulder and Maris kissed it. She gently pushed Lauren's legs farther apart, exploring eagerly with her fingers. Soon, from the repeated, even strokes, Lauren began to moan softly and arch her back. Her red hair brushed against Maris's bare chest and breasts. Lauren's orgasm was strong and repeated itself with a series of shudders as she pressed back against Maris. When she tossed her head again, her hair tickled the scar on Maris's cheek and she felt it tingle. She waited, her fingers still, but touching Lauren. Reluctantly, she pulled her hand away as one last shiver swept through Lauren. The violent toss of her head caught Maris unprepared and she reacted slowly. The back of Lauren's head smashed into the bridge of her nose.

The pain was immediate and intense. "Damn," she said. Blinking back tears, she touched her nose. Her hand came back bloody.

"Oh, Lord, Maris, are you all right?" Lauren faced her.

The dampness, the heat from the water and the physical activity caused a free flow of blood. It streamed down Maris's lips and chin and dripped into the water, briefly staining it pink before the color disappeared and another drop of blood took its place.

"I'm sorry." Lauren seized a washcloth and held it to Maris's nose. "Oh, God, I can't believe I hurt you! I'm so embarrassed."

Maris, her eyes watering, started laughing, "Damn, and you thought I was dangerous with the razor."

Lauren stood in the tub. "Tilt your head back. I hope it's not broken."

"Fuck no, it ain't broke. Maybe cracked a little, but not broken." The telephone rang and Maris said, "Damn, that's probably Amy wanting to know what time we'll be at the party."

"What should I tell her?"

"Tell her you busted my nose in a burst of orgasmic energy and we can't leave until it stops bleeding."

"I'm not going to tell her that." She dashed for the telephone.

Maris drained the water from the bathtub and turned on the shower. The bleeding slowed to a trickle, but her nose felt swollen and sore to touch. She'd ice it down as soon as she showered. Or maybe she'd just get another Miller Lite and hold it to her nose between sips — apply a local and a general at the same time. She hoped the swelling wouldn't be too noticeable.

Chapter Six

Lacey Overstreet bravely volunteered her new home to usher in the new year. Built near a creek where people still picnicked and fished when Maris had lived in the area, the new house was in a rapidly spreading neighborhood in north Austin. It was a beautiful structure with high vaulted ceilings, three bedrooms, two and a half baths, a huge kitchen and a den with a fireplace. The dining room had a hardwood floor excellent for dancing and Lacey had promised to move the table and chairs to the garage before the party.

As they drove to Lacey's, Maris admired Lauren's tight black pants with the matching black blazer with a floral pattern over a white pullover blouse. "You're a heartbreaker tonight."

"Is that good?" Lauren asked, playing with her pearl necklace.

"As long as it's not mine, darling."

"You look good yourself. I'm glad you decided to wear the red shirt."

"Thank you," Maris said. Lauren, complaining that she always wore black and white, had talked her into wearing her new red and white Garth Brooks-style Western shirt.

"You better tell me one more time who'll be here and how they fit together."

"Okay, it's like this. Me, Amy, Kim and Toni all went to college together. Me and Kim were the first to live here in Austin, but I left after I finished training and reported to my duty station in Garland. Shortly after I left, Amy moved here and a few years later Toni followed. The three of them plus a few friends, lovers and ex-lovers' lovers throw the party every year."

"And how many ex-lovers of yours will be here?"

"Hey, girl, don't forget I was on the bench for ten years."

"From before Mary Ann, how many of them will be here?"

"Two, but that's all I'm saying. I don't understand your sudden fascination with my past love life."

Lauren laughed as Maris parked the convertible in

the driveway behind Amy's Jeep Cherokee. "I don't think you intend to tell me anything."

"It must be the FBI in you. First you break my nose and then you grill me about my past. You know it's not polite to kiss and tell."

"We're not talking about kissing. And I'm sorry about your nose."

As they approached the house, sounds of country music and laughter filtered through the front door. The night was cool and damp from the afternoon rain. Lacey and Amy threw open the storm door and waved them inside. Amy was almost as tall as Maris but thinner and less muscular, with shoulder-length straw-colored hair. Lacey, slightly shorter with closely cropped black hair and a stocky build, immediately zeroed in on Lauren's green eyes and red hair. Maris grinned at her, and Lacey slapped her on the shoulder as she stepped across the threshold.

Sarah, Amy's lover of six weeks, was tall, thin and long-legged with wavy blond hair. It was the first time Maris had met her, and she was amused, liking her instantly. She seemed more outgoing and independent than most of Amy's other lovers. Maybe Amy had met her match. Sarah poured Lauren a killer margarita while Maris grabbed a beer out of a cooler on the kitchen floor.

Helping Sarah set up an extra table in the breakfast nook, she didn't see Kim until she slipped in between the table and the wall, pinning her in the corner. Kim kissed her passionately, and Maris tasted the peppermint schnapps on her lips. Pushing her back, Maris smiled. Kim's tight-fitting Levis showed off the curve of her hips and a colorful western shirt, with a denim yoke decorated with silver boots and red peppers, drew attention to her long strawberry blonde hair.

"Hello, Kim, I heard you were back to women these days."

"Oh, Maris, you never forget a damn thing, do you? There was only one man over a decade ago. But, on the other hand, why limit oneself to fishing in one lake?" She squeezed Maris's hand.

Maris shrugged as Toni waved from the doorway and said, "That old argument again. Kim, you know the only *bi* word Maris knows is the one for farewell."

"No, she thinks bi should mean seeing two women at the same time," Kim quipped. The women in the kitchen laughed and Maris, somewhat embarrassed, glanced at Lauren. Kim touched the scar on her right cheek. "I'm glad to see you. Your scar looks much better than it did at Thanksgiving, not nearly as red."

Rubbing off Kim's lipstick, she said, "Let me introduce you and Toni to my lover, Lauren."

As they approached Lauren, Kim said, "What's wrong with your nose? You look like you've been in a fistfight."

Lauren choked on her margarita and grabbed a napkin from a nearby kitchen counter. After wiping her chin, she asked, smiling, "Yeah, honey, what did happen to your nose?"

Maris ignored her and politely made introductions. Toni soon excused herself to organize the music for the night and Kim followed.

Lauren whispered in Maris's ear, "That's one."

Women filled the house and the annual pool

tournament raged in the den. Beer coolers, each labeled with a different brand name, overflowed with ice. Maris, already on her third beer, topped off Lauren's margarita and asked, "Have you seen the rest of the house?"

"No, but I'd like to."

"Come on, I'll give you a tour." Taking her hand, she led her into the room with the pool table. "Have you signed up to play?"

"Are you kidding? You know I don't do sports, and I want to hear about Thanksgiving."

Slowly, they strolled through the house. Maris greeted friends along the way until they reached the dining room with the hardwood floor. Pictures taped to green posterboard documented past parties, camp-outs and rafting trips. A particularly adventuresome trio had snapped photographs of one another in a sky-diving free-fall before jerking open the parachutes. As Lauren stood close to her with a hand on her shoulder, Maris pointed out friends in the photographs.

When she came to the last two photographs, a sharp pain pierced Maris's heart and she wondered if that's what it felt like to be stabbed with a dagger. There, in the last two pictures, was Mary Ann, wearing her teal suit. It was the last Austin party that they attended together, two years ago. Maris stood by her in a black Western-cut jacket, a white shirt, crisply starched jeans and a Christmas tie. She remembered the pictures well. In the first one, they looked startled and were. Dancing alone in Lacey's bedroom at her old house, Maris had slipped a hand inside Mary Ann's blouse about the time the flash went off. Mary Ann was embarrassed and a little angry, more at Maris than the sneaky photographers. To make it up to her, Toni and Amy caught them in front of the fireplace later and took a more proper picture. Taller by one centimeter — she insisted — Mary Ann stood with her head tilted slightly to one side. Her dark brown hair flowed around her shoulders and she smiled at the camera with the sly yet shy grin that had always captivated Maris. She held her breath as if trapped in a vacuum, only dimly aware of time passing and a drop in the crowd noise behind her. She wanted to say something, do something, but the words and action wouldn't come. Oh, Mary Ann, she thought, how can you still make me feel this way? When Lauren's hand dropped from her shoulder, it spurred her into the present. She tore herself away from the pictures and realized that Amy, Lacey, Kim and several other women were watching. She heard Amy ask Lacey, "Who put those pictures up there?"

Lacey said softly, "She didn't know Maris and Mary Ann, and I never thought to tell her."

Maris felt Lauren's arm circle her waist. "She was so beautiful and ya'll were having so much fun. You looked good together." She leaned her head against Maris's shoulder and said, "I see why you loved her so much."

"Like I love you." Maris turned away from the posters and pulled Lauren closer. "How did I get so lucky . . . two women such as you and Mary Ann in one lifetime?"

Lauren wiggled out of her embrace. "Dance with me, lover, before I'm forced to ask Amy."

She glanced back at the pictures as Lauren pulled

her to the improvised dance floor. Lauren inched an arm under her elbow and leaned against her.

She whispered, "It's all right to still love her. I understand."

Maris felt almost crushed by the emotions that erupted within her. Amy and the other women were still watching and she nodded to let them know she was fine. As they joined three other couples dancing to a slow Lori Morgan song, she cleared her throat and said, "I'm glad you're here with me."

The song ended and Lauren said, "I love you so much it scares me." She kissed her. "They're calling you to the pool table. Get us another drink and kick some ass."

By eleven o'clock, the house was jammed with women and a few men. Maris advanced to the quarter finals in pool but lost to a former UT basketball player who went on to win the tournament. Sarah caught her by the arm as she cruised to the beer cooler for another cold one.

"Amy said to tell you if Diane Cooper came. She's here somewhere...I think the front room."

"Thanks, Sarah. I'll find her," Maris said. She looked around for Lauren, caught her eye and signaled for her to follow.

She spotted Diane Cooper in a small group of women in the far corner of the den. Diane, at fifty-five, still managed to surround herself with good-looking women. Her once dark hair was now silver, but her erect back, straight shoulders and graceful, assertive manner hinted at her former athleticism. Maris was a sophomore when Diane returned to college to take a few courses needed to finish a second degree. After graduation she moved to Austin ahead of Maris, Amy and Toni.

Diane smiled broadly when Maris approached. "Maris Middleton, where have you been?" She hugged her.

"Steady working," Maris said. "It's good to see you."

"This is my friend, Darla," Diane said, hugging an attractive woman about fifteen years her junior.

Maris introduced Lauren. "I need to talk to you about a case I'm working. Let's go outside to the patio."

"Sure," Diane said, adding as they stepped out into the cool fresh air, "I was sorry to hear about Mary Ann. I didn't find out until recently."

"Thank you. It was rough for a while." Maris smiled softly at Lauren. "But I'm doing much better now. I wanted to ask you if you remember a woman named Cynthia Allen? She was murdered in 'eighty."

"Yes, it was two years before I returned to school to finish my second degree. I knew her, but not very well. She was Carol's friend."

"I forgot that you and Carol used to be together."

"It was before you and I met. We were together eight years until the bitch dumped me for a bigger paycheck. You know, it was funny — not funny, but odd. Carol knew Cynthia, but I knew the first girl that was killed."

Maris looked at Lauren in surprise. Lauren said, "You knew Debbie Keisler?"

"Yes, we played softball together in summer and

fall league. We partied a lot. It was sad when she was killed. I went to the funeral."

"She was gay?" Maris asked.

"Yes."

"Debbie was married."

"Being married doesn't mean anything."

"That's true," Lauren said. "Nothing in the police report indicated they knew Cynthia or Debbie was gay. Either the investigators didn't realize it or didn't consider it important."

"I doubt if they knew." Diane shrugged.

"Do you remember who Cynthia was with at the time?" Maris asked.

"Don't know her name. She was about ten years older than Cynthia. They were very discreet about their relationship, although they'd go to the bars occasionally. Cynthia was a track coach, but I think she was promoted to assistant principal shortly before she was killed. Carol would remember more — if you could find her — but she's on a cruise with her rich bitch."

"Not bitter, are we?" Maris said, laughing.

"Did you know Debbie Keisler's husband?" Lauren asked.

"Robert? Not really, I'd met him when Debbie first started playing softball."

"Was their breakup friendly?"

"Not at first. He hit her once, shortly after she told him she was a lesbian. He threatened to tell her family and her co-workers. I guess they came to an understanding. They lived in the same house while they looked for a buyer. It seemed to work out better after he found a girlfriend. A sale was pending when she was killed."

Diane's date opened the door to tell them it was almost midnight. Diane went inside and Maris took Lauren's hand. She paused before opening the door. "The police report said nothing about the problems in Debbie's marriage. It could have been important to the investigation and might make her husband a suspect."

"I bet they never found out. Some friends and family might not have even known there were problems with the marriage . . . especially if she still wore her ring. Once he was over his anger, her husband wouldn't want anyone to know his wife was leaving him to be with women. Her lesbian friends, out of loyalty and maybe shock, wouldn't volunteer the information unless asked. Or the investigators may have left it out of the police report as a favor to the family." Lauren tilted her head to the side. "We're assuming that the original investigators were right and Hatcher did it. But husbands have been known to fake sexual homicide."

Maris shook her head. "I don't think these were faked."

"No, I don't either. But rage was a factor. Some men don't take it too well when their wives dump them for a woman. I think we should check out Mr. Keisler."

"Yes, although it's unlikely he's involved." Maris opened the storm door. "It's too big of a coincidence that both women were lesbians. We need to check out Theresa Eastin. Find out if she was. We better get inside or we'll miss the stroke of midnight."

A handsome black woman was passing out champagne in plastic stem glasses. As the grandfather clock in Lacey's den started to sound, someone dimmed the lights and "Auld Lang Syne" played softly. Taking Lauren's glass, Maris sat it on the ledge of the fireplace and said, "A belt buckle polisher. Dance?" When the song ended, she added, "I think we should go soon."

"Have plans, do you?" Lauren smiled and whispered, "Your nose must feel better."

"Yeah, but I . . . I have to get up early tomorrow."

"What's tomorrow?"

"What's tomorrow? Lauren, how in the hell did you get a degree from Notre Dame without knowing something about college football?"

"You don't really want to waste the first day of the New Year watching football, do you?" she teased.

"I don't have to watch all of them. I can listen to some on the radio when we drive home."

"Then you're right, we'd better go. I promise to be through with you by kickoff. But I won't guarantee you'll be well rested."

Chapter Seven

"Do you think you're in any danger?" Ralph Lambert asked as he turned his new desk calendar to the second of January.

"Don't think so," Maris said, leaning back in the gray vinyl chair in Ralph's office at the Pierce County Sheriff's Department. Wayne sat next to her with his long legs stretched out in front of him. Maris noticed he was wearing a new pair of chocolate-brown ostrich boots.

"Why would this guy, assuming he's the same murderer, send you the shoe from one of his first victims and risk bringing attention to himself?" Wayne asked as he studied the box and the black Lovelady shoe. "We certainly hadn't uncovered any connection."

"Lauren thinks he saw me on the news. That's how he knew I was involved in the case. As to why?" She shrugged and shook her head. "Who the hell knows? Maybe he's jacking with us. Maybe he wants to remind us he's gotten away with it for seventeen years. Maybe he wants us to know he's back in business."

Ralph thoughtfully looked at the photocopy of the note. "That doesn't fit with the message he sent you. What does he want you to stay away from?"

"I don't know. Maybe he's afraid that the recent advances in forensics, such as DNA, will ID him." Or he knows I'm a dyke, Maris thought. She sipped her coffee, hoping it would ease her football hangover. She took a slip of paper out of her pocket and handed it to Wayne. "Lauren traced the package using the UPS tracking label. It was sent from the Mail Shoppe in Tyler on December twenty-fourth. She hasn't contacted them yet. Didn't want to step on any toes." Maris shrugged.

Ralph glared at his blank computer screen. "Damn it, if my computer was up we could check on William Roy Hatcher's criminal record. But we've got a guy in here redoing our network system. It's taking him forever to run all of the new cable we need."

"I think I ran into him." Maris rolled her eyes. "He almost knocked me down with a ladder when I came in."

Wayne looked up from his notes. "I'll talk to Austin P.D. about the nineteen eighty murders. Also,

I'll get the Ranger captain to track down the files on the original investigation. I'll talk to the Austin DPS lab about their records and see what evidence they have." He paused to write in the small notebook he always carried. "And I'll contact this Mail Shoppe. Of course, if he used a fake name, address and telephone number —" His pager went off and he tilted it to read the number. "It's an Austin area code." Reaching for the telephone, he dialed a number and after a brief pause identified himself.

Ralph refilled everyone's coffee cup from the pot he kept full whenever he was in his office. "One more bowl game to go," he said, keeping his voice low while Wayne talked on the telephone.

"Yeah, I'm glad too. I never get tired of college ball, but I liked it better when they finished all the bowl games on New Year's Day."

"My wife says the same thing. I —"

"What's your fax number, Ralph?" Wayne asked. He relayed the number and hung up the phone. "Damn, that was Al Wheeler. He's faxing us an article from the *Austin Statesman*. A reporter broke the news in this morning's paper that the 'eighty murder investigation has been reopened and that there was a similar one in Pierce county."

"How could the reporter have found out so soon?" Maris was stunned. Although she had talked to several people in Austin, most were law enforcement professionals or retired professionals. Of the women at the party, only Diane knew that she and Lauren were asking questions about the murders. She didn't want to think Diane would have said anything. "I hope Al doesn't think I tipped them off."

"No, he knows where the leak came from. The

reporter told Al that someone in records told him that the old case files were checked out. He began searching the wires and came across the story in the *Dallas Morning News* about Theresa Eastin's murder. He started putting two and two together and broke the story in this morning's paper."

"Then it'll be in the *Dallas Morning News* by tomorrow," Ralph said.

"Well, guys, I hate it that it came out so soon, but I guess the story's too sensational for us to keep it quiet for long. We still don't know for sure that the murders are by the same person. It could be a copycat who somehow gained possession of the killer's trophies from the nineteen eighty murders." Maris sighed.

"If our killer is on a similar cycle, he should have struck around Christmas," Ralph said.

Wayne frowned. "He may have and we don't know it yet."

Maris drained her Styrofoam coffee cup and dropped it into the trash. "Let me know if anything new comes up." She gathered up the copy of the note and the box with the Lovelady black heel. "I'll keep these with the other evidence and send you a copy of Shannon Stockwell's report. I've got to get home and change so I can be in Fort Worth for court at one. Do you have a copy of the barcodes on the box?"

Wayne nodded and rose to his feet. "What are you doing in court the week of New Year's?"

"It's a strange situation. The case was actually scheduled to go the week before Christmas but a juror got sick and the judge postponed. He wants to finish it this week because of a big civil case starting Monday."

Wayne rubbed his chin thoughtfully. "Be careful. This guy knows where you live. And after the newspaper reports, he'll know we're looking into the nineteen eighty murders. You have any prowlers or anything, you call nine-one-one and then me or Ralph. Okay?"

"Don't worry, Wayne. If he comes nosing around my place, Earnhardt'll tear his leg off. Then I'll shoot his ass. If all else fails, we'll sic the FBI on him."

Maris circled the new Justice Center in Fort Worth one more time, searching for a parking place. Located on Belknap and Taylor streets, catty-cornered to the police department, the facilities were a vast improvement over the old courthouse where witnesses waited to testify in tiny closet-like rooms piled high with dusty file boxes and broken furniture. Unfortunately, the parking situation was worse since more of the street parking was reserved for police vehicles. She could park at the Tandy Center, but it was expensive. Instead, she opted to park at Shannon's office and walk to court, since she had to go there anyway to pick up the report and photographs.

The walk from Shannon's took her about fifteen minutes. No judge or jury was in the courtroom when she arrived. The defense table was empty and one man sat at the prosecution table. She frowned, thinking that court had been canceled and she hadn't been notified. Walking to the rail, she said, "Excuse me. Is the Sanchez case still set for today?"

"Are you the chemist?" He leapt to his feet extending his hand.

"Yes, I'm Maris Middleton." His height surprised her. He would have towered over Wayne Coffey. She guessed he was at least six-ten or -eleven and wondered if he'd played college basketball. He engulfed her hand with a firm handshake.

"I'm Nick Hearn. I talked to you on the phone. We're almost ready to go. The judge had to make a phone call and then they'll bring in the jury. We're under the rule. I guess you know what that means?"

She nodded. She'd only heard it explained about two hundred times. The rule prohibited witnesses from talking to one another or to anyone else — except for the lawyers involved in the trial — about the case or their testimony. They also were not allowed in the courtroom until it was time for them to testify. Nick opened the gate for her and she followed him past the empty jury box through a door in the back of the room. They entered a bright open area partitioned into small offices. Behind the last wall were two tables and eight chairs in a break room with restrooms and water fountain nearby. Two officers she recognized were reading the paper at one table.

She fell into an easy conversation with them and within minutes the first officer was called to testify. She opened her case folder and studied her notes. The case involved a narcotics buy/bust and four kilos of cocaine. Ten guns and almost fifty thousand dollars in cash had been seized. Maris had returned the evidence to the submitting agency after she weighed and analyzed the cocaine. The main officer in the case had brought it to court with him that morning and it would be in there when she testified. The next two witnesses played minor roles in the

71

investigation and their testimonies were short. Within an hour, the bailiff called Maris's name.

She felt the rush of adrenaline as always when she followed the bailiff into the courtroom. It was not nerves but rather excitement, anticipation, like coming to bat in a close ballgame with the team counting on you to get the big hit. She casually glanced at the mostly female jury. The fourth juror in the first row, a blond in a sharp navy blue dress, caught her eye and flashed her a knowing smile. Wondering if she was interpreting it correctly, Maris turned to face the judge. She'd never been in this judge's courtroom before, but his appearance and mannerisms were impressive. He was black, about fifty to fifty-five years old, with the shoulders and chest of a defensive lineman. His voice was a rich baritone that boomed throughout the courtroom when he asked her to raise her right hand.

"Do you solemnly swear to tell the truth, the whole truth, and nothing but the truth, so help you God?"

"I do," Maris said, projecting her best court voice. She climbed the two steps into the witness box, slid into the leather chair and adjusted the microphone.

When she was settled, the prosecutor said, "Please state your name."

"Maris Middleton."

The prosecutor quickly ran through the usual questions about her educational background, training and experience to establish her as an expert witness in the identification of controlled substances. Maris always tried to use these questions to establish a rapport with the jury, to study the defense attorney and to relax on the stand before the more difficult testimony started. Occasionally, when she looked at the jury, the blond on the first row would catch her attention and smile shyly before averting her eyes. Maris tried to remember if she knew her from somewhere but was sure she didn't. It left her slightly unsettled to think that the blond might be flirting with her in open court. She turned her attention to the prosecutor when he approached the bench.

"Are these the items you received from Officer Blandon?"

"Yes, they are. I recognize my case number and initials on the packages."

"What did you do with them next?"

"I checked the items to make sure they were in a sealed condition and I —"

"Were they sealed?"

"Yes, sir."

"Then, what did you do?"

"I gave them a laboratory number unique to the items in this case and —" A siren wailed and then an alarm began clanging.

The tall prosecutor turned to the bailiff, who shrugged and went out a side door. "What is that, Your Honor? Should I continue?" he asked.

The judge held up his hand as a computerized voice said, "This is an emergency. Please exit the building immediately using the stairwell. Do not use the elevators. Do not panic. Please exit the building in an orderly fashion. This is an emergency." It began to repeat the message.

The bailiff returned and said, "Your Honor, the alarm is real. We're supposed to leave."

Just my luck, Maris thought, fifteen more minutes

and she probably would have been finished. She turned to the judge.

"Okay, ladies and gentlemen. Let's go. Proceed to the sidewalk directly across the street on the west side and wait there. Remember not to discuss the case amongst yourselves or with anyone else. Bailiffs, one of you take the defendant. The other see to the jury. Let's go, young lady," he added, looking at Maris. "I guess we'll take a little break."

Taking her records and briefcase, Maris left the witness stand. The prosecutor was packing the drugs into a large cardboard box. The defendant and defense attorney were already gone and most of the jury had filed out of the courtroom. She helped the prosecutor carry the drugs and guns to a vault in the clerk's office before walking down four flights of stairs. She saw the case officers standing on the sidewalk and loped across the street.

"Okay, which of you guys had an early date and pulled the fire alarm?" she asked.

Before they could answer the judge approached. "Since it's already three-thirty, I'm going to adjourn court for the day. Be back here at nine o'clock in the morning. I've already told the jury. Have you seen the prosecutor?"

"Yes, sir," Maris said. "He's crossing the street now."

The judge went to meet him and Maris said good-bye to the officers. She circled the courthouse, keeping the width the street away from it as per instructions from the deputies. Several hook and ladder trucks had arrived and firemen were searching the building. Once upon a time, these incidents were assumed to be pranks, but that was before the Oklahoma City explosion. She hurried to Shannon's office. Maybe she could talk her into a happy hour. Before the office came into view, she was assaulted by the acrid odor of burning plastic and rubber. Thick black smoke drifted across Belknap. Turning the corner at Jones, she saw the smoke billowing out of her pickup. The passenger-side door was open with the window shattered, and a fireman stood by the seat, squeezing the trigger on a fire extinguisher.

"Goddamn," she mumbled, running to the truck. The flames were out, but smoke filled the cab of the pickup. She saw Shannon and Timothy watching from a window. After waving to them, she introduced herself to the fireman in charge and to the Fort Worth police officer.

"You're lucky," the officer said. "The receptionist inside this office saw the fire and reported it before it got very bad. Looks like you can get by with a new seat and a good cleaning."

"Son-of-a-bitch," Maris said looking in through the driver's side door. On the damaged vinyl seat near a pile of fine paper ashes were the remnants of a book of matches and a cigarette butt. It was a crude but effective arson delay mechanism that works when the cigarette burns down far enough to ignite the match heads, which in turn set fire to the shredded newspaper.

"You better look at the back of your camper shell," a fireman said.

Maris trotted to the rear of the truck. A dead kitten was tied to the bumper and across the back glass of the camper door was a message written in white shoe polish. In three-inch letters, it read, *I can find you anywhere. Stay the fuck away.*

"Do you know anything about this?" the officer asked.

"Yes, I'm afraid I do." She gave the officer one of her cards. "This incident may be related to at least one capital murder." She explained as briefly as possible about the Pierce county murder and the first threatening note she received. "We're going to need a complete investigation — fingerprints, so forth. I better call Wayne Coffey. He's the Texas Ranger in charge of the case." She wondered if her harasser had also set off the alarm at the courthouse.

Her first telephone call was to Lauren. She told her to make sure Earnhardt was kept inside unless one of them was there to watch him — just in case. Lauren agreed to go by the house and bring him in before coming to Fort Worth to get her. Maris would call her mobile phone and let her know where to pick her up. Her second call was to Wayne Coffey. They decided to let Fort Worth P.D. process the truck for evidence. He and Ralph were both concerned for Maris's safety, but she thought her new playmate would have already attacked her if he was inclined to do so. The truck was too smoky for Maris to drive and she made a third call to a body shop in Allen and made arrangements for them to tow the truck back for repairs as soon as the P.D. finished with it.

By four-thirty, Maris and Shannon were leaning on the worn mahogany bar at a cop hangout not far from the courthouse. It was crowded with courthouse personnel who lucked into an early quitting time — thanks to Maris and her pen pal. Shannon bought the first round, and as the bartender set her drink in front of her, Maris pondered the messages, wondering exactly what he was warning her away from. By the second beer, her thoughts had turned to Lauren and what she would think of Shannon. Turning to Shannon, she laughed and said, "You'll never guess what happened to me today in court. I think one of the jurors was flirting with me. And she was pretty, too."

Chapter Eight

One hundred feet from the highway, the brunette lay immodestly under the sycamore tree with her dark green dress hiked to her waist, exposing her mutilated genitalia. The shiny, white bone in the stump on her left hand gleamed obscenely in the light that filtered through the bare branches. And the sharp point of her two inch left heel pointed at Maris like the icy finger of an angel of death. Mocking the sudden theft of life, the cherry-red fingernails on her right hand added a sparkle of personality to the corpse and hinted at the permanent loss of a spirited and vibrant individual. Maris shivered in her black fatigues, as much from the coldness of violent death as from the cool morning air. Focusing her camera, she snapped another photograph. Ralph's call at four a.m. on Sunday, January 5th, summoned her to the lonely two-lane highway where they waited for sunrise before entering the crime scene.

"Now we know what he wanted you — us — to stay away from," Wayne said grumpily. "It's a good thing you got your pickup back."

"Yes, the body shop did a rush job for me and had it ready late yesterday afternoon. How'd you find the body?"

"Two drunks stumbled on it last night. I suspect they were planning to steal some trees for firewood. We've had several complaints about that lately." He pointed to some scattered skeletal remains of another victim a few yards away. "I don't think they saw that one."

She returned to her work after he walked over to talk to Ralph. She focused on the muddy, leaf-infested ground around the brunette's thighs. Her job was to document and recover the shoeprint evidence, and they were in luck. The ground, damp from a heavy rain on the third, betrayed the killer's path from the side of the two-lane highway to the grove of trees. The killer left many shoeprints — some only partials due to the heavy foliage surrounding the body — as he calmly positioned the victim and her clothing before committing the last atrocity by mutilating her vagina.

Maris numbered each shoeprint and marked it with a yellow flag to prevent another investigator from accidentally stepping on it. Working quickly, she sketched the direction of travel and location of each one. After the entire area was photographed, including examination-quality closeups of each impression, Maris poured dental stone casts of the deeper, more complete prints. The tread pattern indicated a hiking or military boot designed for good traction. From the brunette, the prints were interrupted for several feet by heavy leaves and brush before they wandered back into the woods several yards to the skeletal remains of the second body. These remains, ravished and scattered by carnivores and insects, consisted of only bones and some strands of tattered clothing. A few stray blond hairs littered the ground around the skull.

"Wayne," she called when she saw the big man cross the clearing. When he came over, she said, "He was in no hurry to leave. It's like he stood here to visit her. Maybe he got off, fantasizing, reliving her death."

"I'd like to get my hands on this sick bastard. Just for a few minutes."

Farther down the trail, Ralph crashed through the scrub oak and said, "Goddamn, we've got another badly decomposed body, mostly bones near another skeleton back here. What is this? His fucking dumping grounds?"

"Possessions," she said. Suddenly, she understood completely. "It makes sense. This is his collection — his women. The left ring finger traditionally bears the engagement ring or wedding ring. Both are considered symbols of unavailability and, to some, ownership. These are his women, his possessions, and he wanted them all here together. If we'd known what we'd find here, we could have set up surveillance and caught him coming back."

"It's too fucking late now." Wayne jerked off his gray felt Stetson and ran his hand through his hair. "I wonder why he left Theresa Eastin somewhere else."

"Something to think about," Maris said.

Ralph frowned. "I still don't understand why he sent the warnings to Maris. If he views the victims as his possessions, it looks like he would feel more threatened by another male. Why didn't he send warnings to me or Wayne? Both of us were on the news and quoted in the newspaper."

Maris had the sinking feeling that she knew the answer. If the victims were all lesbians, she was the bigger threat in the killer's twisted view. Soon she'd have to let Ralph and Wayne know her suspicions.

Making a list in his small spiral notebook, Wayne said, "We've got to get more help out here, expand the crime scene and divide it into grids. Search each one for bones, body parts, scraps of clothing or anything else we can find. I'd better call the pathologist in Tyler. Wait until the fucking press finds out we have four sets of remains out here."

"That we know of," Maris added. "While you get organized, I'll continue to process the shoeprints. I'll have the casts up and out of the way by the time we're ready to start the recovery process."

Two and a half hours later, using a black indelible marker, Maris labeled the back of the last shoeprint cast after she lifted it from the ground. Luckily, the dental stone hardened rapidly, allowing her to stack the shoeprint casts carefully in a cardboard box and lock them in the camper of the pickup.

Afterwards, she walked the gravel shoulder of the road near the path to the brunette's body and searched for tire tracks, cigarette butts or other items of interest. She found nothing. It was almost noon, and she'd been on site for several hours. Increasingly aware of the need to relieve herself, she searched for someplace away from the crime scene. She spotted a thick copse of scrub oak and tall, dried grass across the highway about two hundred feet from the police cars parked on the shoulder. Hurriedly, she trotted down the side of the road, skirting a soft patch of fresh asphalt. Placing one hand on top of a cedar post and using the other to push down the top strand of barbed wire, she vaulted over the fence. Lowering her trousers, she squatted on the ground. After using a napkin from her pocket, she guiltily dropped it on the damp ground and stepped away to button her black fatigues.

The temperature, still in the low forties, chilled Maris. Given a choice, she'd rather be hot than cold, but the cool temperatures helped keep down the odor. She wished she had a cup of coffee to warm her hands.

After jumping the fence, she stretched and started to cross the highway. Looking at the ground, she froze in her steps. On the very edge of the asphalt patch near the gravel shoulder were four cigarette butts, two of them pressed into the black surface in a partial shoeprint impression identical in tread design to the ones near the bodies. Kneeling, she read *EAGLE* in reverse print on a label in the instep of the impression. *Marlboro*, she read on the filter tips of the cigarette butts. She touched the black asphalt, expecting it to feel sticky. The patch felt oily but was completely dry and hard. The shoeprint must have been left shortly after the patch was poured.

Her heart pounded as she jogged across the highway to find Wayne. She knew why the bastard dumped Theresa Eastin west of town instead of here with the others — a highway work crew was no doubt patching potholes in the road. He'd watched and waited, fretting they'd find his women, until he became impatient or frightened and left. If they could find out when the crew had been scheduled to work, they might know exactly what day he dumped Theresa Eastin's body. If they were lucky, one of the workers might remember seeing a vehicle and provide a description of it and the driver. The odor of fresh tar and the age of the remains must have kept the crew from smelling anything.

Excitedly, Maris and Ralph photographed the cigarette butts and shoeprint. After much discussion, they cut the section of asphalt containing the shoe-print out of the road bed after Maris made a cast of it. Wayne and Ralph collected the cigarette butts and gave them to Maris for possible DNA typing of the saliva residue. The PCR method that Maris used was more than sensitive enough to type the DNA in the epithelial cells found in saliva residue unless the recent rain and the asphalt interfered.

Around two o'clock, someone brought a sack of cold, soggy hamburgers and limp french fries from town along with a case of Cokes. Starving, Maris thought the food was delicious and devoured hers quickly. More help arrived with stakes and twine to form the search grids. When they were finished, Wayne divided the officers into three teams with himself, Ralph and Maris as team leaders. By dusk, the body and most of the skeletal remains had been recovered. It was decided that only Ralph and his team would return the next morning for a final daylight search of the area.

Maris was cold, hungry and depressed when she stopped at the Dairy Queen in Pierce to wash her hands and grab a cup of coffee to help her stay awake for the hour-and-a-half drive home. She looked forward to a hot shower and a warm spot in bed next to Lauren.

Chapter Nine

Maris slept late, waiting until ten o'clock to start calling sources of information. Two dozen calls later, she located an Army-Navy store in McKinney that sold Eagle boots. Thirty minutes later, she entered the store with one of the better shoeprint casts from the scene. Her task was easier than she expected. There was only one style, one model of Eagle boot, and they came in only one color — black. The sole of the boot consisted of cross-shaped lugs covering the ball-of-the-foot area and forming a semi-circle around the single lug in the heel. The name, EAGLE, was in a rectangular box in the instep. When she held the shoeprint cast up next to the boot, the patterns were identical.

Whoever her suspect was, he wore Eagle Sniper/ Commando Special boots, probably size twelve. Identifying the style of the boots was the easy part. The difficult task was proving that only the suspect's footwear could have made the impressions found at the crime scene. Sometimes it couldn't be done. In this case, it would be easy. She'd noticed a repeating accidental characteristic in several · of the shoeprints found at the scene — a deep cut on the third grid up from the logo in the instep of the left boot. It was unlikely that another pair of Eagle boots of the same size would have a cut in the same location of the same length and depth. If they located a suspect and found his boots, she could put the boots at the scene.

Deep in thought, Maris jumped when the sales clerk said over her shoulder, "Important case, huh?"

Maris whirled and found herself staring into a large purple bubble before it popped and disappeared behind a row of incredibly straight white teeth. She realized, after falling back a step, that the girl behind the bubblegum was really quite pretty. Her almost jet-black hair was cut extremely short, and she wore black fingernail polish and dark red lipstick. Three earrings pierced one ear and two the other, but somehow she must have resisted the temptation to pierce her nose or tongue. Since she was only sixteen or seventeen, maybe her parents had nixed any more piercings. A small tattoo, a blue dolphin, adorned her inner left wrist. An attractive teenager, she'd someday make a beautiful woman.

Maris quickly introduced herself and added, "I'm

working on a murder case, and I need to find out as much about these boots as possible. You must be the one I talked to on the phone this morning."

"Yeah, I was the only one here. I'm Rhonda. What can I tell you about the boots?"

"For starters, is this the only place in town that carries them?"

"Actually we're one of only two stores in Texas that sells them. Us and one in Houston, but they can be ordered by catalogue. I can't remember the name . . . Oh, here's Mr. McDaniel, the store manager. He can tell you."

Hearing his name, Mr. McDaniel, a stooped, bald-headed man, stopped and looked at Maris. He raised his eyebrows when he saw the shoeprint cast. Looking through the lower half of his bifocals, he examined the cast while the clerk explained what Maris wanted.

"U. S. Militia, Weapons and Essential Equipment, that's the name of the catalogue company. My store and the one in Houston made a deal with the manufacturer twenty-five years ago, shortly before exclusive rights were given to the catalogue company."

"Do you sell a lot of them?"

"Funny thing, used to sell them only by special order. To police SWAT teams, mostly. Also, these militia types, men you'd expect to be in the KKK or American Nazi Party. We'd sell maybe five pair a year. They last forever, almost can't wear them out. I use them for hunting and fishing. Lately all the kids want them — seems like they caught on with the dirt look."

"Grunge, Mr. McDaniel." The clerk giggled.

"Whatever. They've made these boots for twenty-five years, exactly the same way. Overnight every kid wants a pair. Girls wear them with dresses and shorts. The manufacturer, after all these years, started making smaller sizes just for women. Girls wanted other colors, but they still come only in black. The company claims that once you wear an Eagle boot you won't wear any other kind. Want a catalogue to take with you?"

"Yes, I'd appreciate that."

With a nod he walked away and Rhonda whispered, "They're on the way out now, you know . . . with the kids. But he's right, the police, outdoorsmen and military types love them."

"I guess murderers like them too," Maris said. She thanked Mr. McDaniel for the catalogue and requested permission to photograph a pair of size-twelve boots.

After she returned to the lab, Maris called and left a message with the Highway Patrol secretary for Wayne to call her. She was pleased to have already identified the type of boots that made the shoeprints at the scene. With that out of the way, she'd be free to analyze any evidence recovered by the medical examiner's office during the course of the autopsies. She was halfway finished with the report when someone rang the doorbell at the lab entrance. She expected an officer with evidence to submit, but when she looked through the security hole, she saw a woman, about fifty to fifty-five, dressed comfortably in faded blue jeans and a blue cotton long-sleeved shirt draped over a white turtleneck sweater. Slender, with silver hair, the woman smiled when Maris opened the door.

"Maris Middleton, I presume." Her hazel eyes swept over her and Maris thought she saw a glint of amusement when the woman extended her hand. "I'm Barbara Shelton."

Maris took it. "Please come in. I've been intending to call you." She was taller than Maris expected and more athletic in appearance.

"Edward Evers called me on New Year's Day and told me about your visit. I thought you'd call me, but after reading the newspaper this morning, I couldn't wait. I hope I'm not interrupting your work at a bad time."

"No," Maris said, leading her through the lab into the den. "I was about to break for a late lunch. Would you care to join me for a sandwich or something to drink?"

"Something to drink would be great. You have a well-equipped lab, clean and neat."

"Thank you. Iced tea okay?" As Barbara nodded, Earnhardt charged into the room from the hallway, barking furiously. "A little late, aren't you?" Maris said. "Must have caught you sleeping on the bed again." He ran over to Barbara, sniffing her pant leg and shoes. Maris got after him and went into the kitchen to prepare the tea.

Barbara said, "I assume that the Rangers are looking for William Roy Hatcher." Bitterness sounded in her voice. "I've always feared the murders would start again. Lucia, my partner, is a captain with Fort Worth P.D., and she's kept a vigilant watch for similar murders — victims missing a left hand, any victims with painted nails, black heels — throughout

89

the country. Until Theresa Eastin's body was found, she hadn't heard of anything similar. After all this time, I doubted a connection until Edward described the shoe you received."

"Now you're sure?" Maris asked handing her a Mason jar full of tea.

"Aren't you?"

"It seems almost unbelievable that we have a guy resuming a string of murders after seventeen years. But I think they're related — one way or another. Mind if we walk outside with Earnhardt, Lauren and I have been afraid to leave him out alone since I've been getting the threats and my truck was set on fire." She explained to Barbara about the harassment. "Silly to worry, I guess."

"No, not silly. In fact you'd better think about your own safety." Barbara followed Maris and Earnhardt outside. After they were seated in the lawn chairs, she said, "About what you said a while ago. If you're thinking copycat by someone with inside knowledge of the Austin murders, it's not."

"Someone could find a similar pair of black Lovelady heels if he knew what he was looking for and looked hard enough, long enough."

"He would have to really know what to look for." Maris shifted in her lawn chair to get a better look at Barbara. She met Maris's gaze. "I was the first woman chemist hired by DPS. I was proud of that and I did a good job." She took a sip of the iced tea. "It didn't come out at the time, but Cynthia Allen was my lover."

"It must have been very difficult for you, a nightmare." Maris shook her head. "I don't think anyone's told me how and when she disappeared." Maris wanted to hear it from Barbara. Maybe she knew something that wasn't in the police report.

"She was abducted from the parking lot at the hotel downtown where she was attending a school sports banquet."

"Did she wear dresses or skirts with heels often?"

"She'd recently been promoted to assistant principal at a junior high school and wore dress clothes almost every day." Barbara massaged her temple. "Hearing about those bodies has given me a terrific headache. I guess it hurts to remember. The last time I saw her, we had an argument. It was two days before she was killed. We attended a friend's anniversary party at the bar in Austin." Barbara looked away. "She wanted to buy a house together and I refused. I said I didn't want my parents to know I was gay. I was worried about my job. Sounds foolish, doesn't it? My only excuse is that I hadn't been out very long at the time. I didn't even know she was missing until they called us to work the crime scene. It actually took me a minute to recognize her. When I did, I should have excused myself from the case, but I thought I was the best available to do the job. As it was, a rookie police officer stepped on a partial shoeprint and destroyed it before we could make a cast or even take examination-quality photographs. Looking back, I don't understand my reaction. I should have run out of that clearing screaming. I should have fallen apart but didn't. I don't understand how I managed to get through it. I couldn't do it now."

"Sometimes we do what we have to do. And it

helps that the shock protects us." It was cool on the patio, and they went back inside once Earnhardt was ready.

"I'd like to say the shock helped, but I don't know. I don't think I even believed it was her at first. Edward and Bill Rogers did most of the work near the body. The lab work was the easy part. There I could pretend it was just another case. I don't think the reality of her death hit me until days afterwards."

"When I lost my lover, Mary Ann, I was numb for weeks. Grief deadens the senses."

"It may sound noble — the grief-stricken lover who immerses herself in work to help find her lover's murderer. Truthfully, I was in hiding. I couldn't even bring myself to acknowledge our relationship enough to take responsibility for the funeral. It was planned by her friends from school. It's an old-fashioned word, but in the end, she was forsaken. I let her down."

"I think you're being too hard on yourself."

Barbara leaned back on the sofa and crossed her legs. "I don't think I'm hard enough. Once the investigation fizzled, I couldn't stand to go to work. I quit DPS and went to IBM. It was a good job, but I kept running into people, things and places that reminded me of her. And I couldn't get that bastard, William Roy, out of my mind. We knew he did it, but his daddy squirreled him away in some exclusive drug-rehab center. The fingernail was the only real evidence we had. When we examined his hands, the nails were freshly clipped and manicured. No chance of a physical match on the torn edges. Might have matched the striations on the nails, but we didn't even have enough probable cause for a search warrant. No DNA typing was available yet." Barbara shrugged. "I decided to leave Austin and accepted a teaching position at the Osteopathic College in Fort Worth. Occasionally, I'll help the Tarrant County M.E.'s office with a research project. That's as close as I care to get to forensic work anymore."

"Did you know that Debbie Keisler was also a lesbian?"

Barbara's jaw dropped and she shook her head. "Are you sure? She was married, living with her husband. I never heard any rumors about her."

"I found out by accident."

"It seems an extraordinary coincidence that both victims were gay. What are the odds on that?"

"Huge — if it's a coincidence." Maris frowned. "Once DNA typing became available, why wasn't the case reopened?"

"We tried. In fact, I think we tried too soon. DNA was too new to the Texas courts. We couldn't get a judge to grant a court order for a sample from Hatcher without a grand jury indictment. As we were getting ready to present the case to them, the Texas Ranger in charge was killed in the line of duty. It threw everything into disarray. On top of that, the Austin detective wasn't well. The grand jury refused to indict due to the lack of sufficient evidence. I was devastated. I thought DNA would solve all our problems." She sighed. "We tried to get the Attorney General's office to launch an independent investigation but failed. As time went by, I took comfort in the fact that there were no other murders. At least, Senator Hatcher kept his son under control and, from what I hear, in and out of drug rehab and mental institutions. That hell is almost as bad as prison. That thought has probably kept me from killing him."

"The partial shoeprint that was lost — do you remember what it looked like?"

"It was some kind of hiking boot, maybe a military boot. There was a partial name in the instep area. Couldn't read it, but it looked like it started with an *E* or *B*. If I remember correctly, some of the lab photographs show the shoeprint, but they're all at a bad angle."

"I want you to look at something," Maris said, placing her jar of iced tea on the coffee table. She stepped into the lab and returned with one of the better shoeprint casts from the crime scene.

"Seems like I remember cross-shaped tread something like this. You don't expect him to be wearing the same pair of shoes after all these years?"

"No, but he might always wear the same brand. I have a friend that won't wear anything but Justin boots." She set the cast on the floor. "Did Cynthia wear a ring on her left hand?"

"I gave her a ring on our first Valentine's Day. Funny, I could give her a ring but wouldn't move in with her or let her move in with me."

"Did anything unusual occur at the bar when ya'll went to the anniversary party?"

"Other than our quarrel, no."

"Were they having any problems at the bar, in the parking lot?"

"Like gay-bashing? No, not that I'm aware of. We were in separate cars, and because of our argument, we both went home to our own apartments. She told a mutual friend that she was so upset she didn't realize she was speeding until Austin P.D. stopped her and gave her a speeding ticket."

"I saw the speeding ticket in her purse." Leaning forward, she said, "I don't think it's a coincidence that both women were lesbians. I think he knew it and it's one of the reasons he chose them as victims. His second criteria was the feminine look . . . the painted nails, black high-heeled shoes."

"What about your new victims? Are they lesbians?"

"I don't know yet. My lover is an FBI agent and she's looking into Theresa Eastin's background. We'll check the other victims when they're ID'd. If they are, I'll have to tell the Rangers what I know."

"Does that bother you?"

"Not really. My personal life is no secret, but I don't advertise it either. If it's true, it'll impact the psychological profile of the killer, especially concerning his motives — what drives his rage toward these women."

"I know it's a lot to ask, but I'd appreciate it if you'd keep me informed about the investigations."

"No promises, but I'll do what I can. I appreciate your coming by to talk to me. We'll get him, whoever it is."

"I know who it is and it's not a copycat. It's not someone else. It's Hatcher."

Long after Barbara left, her words echoed in Maris's ears. Barbara was so damned certain it was Hatcher. She still didn't understand why he risked bringing attention to himself by sending her one of his souvenirs, threatening her and vandalizing her truck. If it wasn't for the presence of the semen in the shoe, Maris would suspect that someone, maybe even Barbara, who wanted the 1980 murders re-opened might be creating the mischief. But that made about as much sense as roping a bobcat. Why wouldn't they just pick up the telephone and call Wayne or the Pierce County Sheriff's Office? Maybe he really was simply warning her away from his women.

She worked on the first of four rush cocaine cases so she could fax the results to the officer involved. Two were preliminary buys and the officer wanted to buy larger quantities if the drugs were real. Two other cases involved civil seizures of money and vehicles. When she still hadn't heard from Wayne after faxing the last of the drug results to the waiting officers, she called the Pierce County Sheriff's Office. Catching Ralph at his desk, she described the Eagle Sniper/Commando boots to him and suggested a court order to obtain catalogue records from the U. S. Militia, Weapons, and Essential Equipment Company. If he or Wayne could find some computer whiz to cross-reference the name of a customer who lived in Austin in '79 or '80 with one who now lived in northeast Texas and still ordered Eagle boots, they might have a suspect.

Hanging up the phone, Maris glanced at the clock. It was almost seven-thirty and she was concerned that Lauren wasn't home yet. Then she remembered that she'd joined a gym downtown. Restless, she threw on an old Aggie T-shirt and pair of sweats, strode to her weight room and flew into a vigorous workout routine. Finishing at a quarter after nine, she collapsed in her lounge chair with a glass of ice water, moments before she heard Lauren's key turn the lock. Earnhardt rushed to meet her.

Wearing a flashy new purple windsuit, she bent to kiss Maris before going to the fireplace to leave her purse and Sig P228 nine-millimeter pistol on the mantel. "What did you do today, lover? You look as tired and sweaty as I feel."

"Besides thinking about you, I identified the boots that left the shoeprints near the bodies. It helped that I found the partial in the asphalt with the Eagle name."

"The biggest cases sometimes are solved on the luckiest breaks."

"True. Barbara Shelton dropped by this afternoon. You were right. She and Cynthia Allen were lovers."

"How sad for her. I can't imagine investigating my lover's murder."

"And I hope you don't have to."

"I'll bet. I did some checking in my spare time. Theresa Eastin was probably gay. She was co-mortgager with another woman on a condominium on McKinney Avenue in Dallas."

"The FBI spying on innocent citizens again," Maris teased. "Let's fix grilled cheese sandwiches or something quick, take a shower and go to bed."

"You must be tired — it's not even ten yet."

"Not tired," Maris said, taking Lauren's hand. "Lonely."

It felt like she'd been asleep forever when the telephone shrieked and she bolted to the side of the bed. Her heart pounding, Maris grabbed the receiver and blurted hoarsely, "Hello." Glancing at the sickly green glow of the alarm clock, she saw that it was only midnight. She couldn't have slept for more than thirty minutes. With concern, she recognized Shannon's voice.

"It's Buster. He's down and I can't get him up."

Maris heard a sharp crack in the background. "What the fuck was that?"

"Thunder. We're having a hell of a storm. If I don't get him on his feet, he'll get pneumonia. I hated to call you but I can't find Robin. I didn't know who else to call."

"Don't worry. I'll be out there as soon as I can." After hanging up the phone, Maris clicked on a night-light and turned to Lauren. "It's Shannon's horse — the one I told you about. I have to go help her. That goddamn Robin must be out fucking around again."

"You want me to go with you?"

"No need both of us being tired tomorrow." Maris threw on a pair of jeans and a flannel shirt. Sitting on the side of the bed, she pulled on a pair of socks.

"Maris, I need to ask you something."

"No, I don't think the Cowboys will make it to the Super Bowl this year." Maris struggled into her work boots and stood. She bent to kiss Lauren and realized that the question must be serious. Kneeling, she asked, "What is it, honey?"

"Should I be worried about you and Shannon?"

"Of course not."

"Are you sure? She has that damsel-in-distress attraction."

Maris kissed Lauren's forehead. "Yes, and she deserves someone like me." She laughed. "I'm teasing. You see, some red-headed FBI agent snared me a while back. I've got to go, honey." Maris stood. "Try to go back to sleep."

Maris parked her truck in front of the barn and ran through a deluge to a side door. She scanned the barn and saw Shannon standing in front of an open stall. She walked past four other stalls of restless snorting horses, including a mare with what looked like a very young foal.

"Goddamn it, Buster, get up," Shannon implored, jerking on his halter. The sorrel quarter horse snorted and rolled over on his back, kicking. His forefeet lashed out dangerously close to Shannon.

"Be careful, girl." Maris pulled her back away from the writhing horse. "Colic?"

"Yes, I've got to get him up before he twists a bowel."

"You called the vet?"

"I took him yesterday. He was having mild colic then. The vet also found an infected tooth. He missed it when I took him last week. The tooth is why he's been so sick lately. It made it hard for him to eat and caused the colic. The vet pulled it and put him on some strong antibiotics. Overall he's healthy and should be fine once he recovers from the infection. I thought he was over the colic and we were on the downhill side. Luckily a strange noise woke me up after I went to bed."

Maris was concerned. "What kind of noise?"

"At first, I thought it was Robin. Should have known better. When I didn't see her truck, I started

down the stairs to investigate and heard someone at
my back door. I got scared and ran to my room and
called the sheriff's office. It looks like someone tried
to break in. The deputy theorized whoever it was
thought I was gone since I went to bed so early and
the house was quiet. He took a report and I asked
him to check the barn with me. I'm glad that I did
because I found Buster down in his stall. The deputy
was going to help me, but he was called to work a
bad wreck."

"Why didn't you tell me over the phone that
someone tried to break in?"

"I guess I was more worried about Buster."

The attempted break-in bothered Maris, but she
turned her attention to the horse. "Did the vet give
you anything for him?"

"Yes, I gave it to him over an hour ago. Mineral
oil to help with the impaction and some Banamine
for pain. The vet says that if the colic returned he
might have a twist in one of the intestines or an
impaction that's not moving. Sometimes it can only
be relieved by surgery and the surgery survival rate
is only about fifty percent in young horses. At his
age, it's almost nil. I'm not putting him through
that. We need to walk him for twenty minutes, then
rest him ten, unless he's trying to roll, give him
water in small amounts and hope for the best. If he's
not out of it in five or six hours, we'll have to put
him down." She glanced at her watch. "Thanks for
coming. I knew I couldn't handle him alone."

"I'm glad you called. He seems to be in less pain
already. Maybe the pain killer is working."

"I hope so."

The horse had stopped thrashing and stretched out on his side, although his breathing was labored. Shannon grabbed one side of the halter and Maris the other. Buster groaned and struggled to rise. His front feet slipped on the straw before he found his footing and came to his feet. His head drooped wearily when Maris clasped the lead line to his halter. The rear of the barn opened into a small arena with a training corral where they could walk him and stay dry. They could hear the rain pounding on the metal roof. Occasionally lightning flashed illuminating the barn followed by rolling thunder that shook the window panes and made Buster more uneasy.

After they'd walked him for several minutes, one on each side, Maris said, "Let me take him for a while. You go rest." Their boots sank in the soft dirt of the corral with each step and walking was hard going.

Shannon jumped up on the fence and checked her watch again. "Let's give him another ten minutes and then we'll put him up. You haven't asked about Robin."

"I figured you'd tell me what you wanted me to know."

"There's not much to tell. She didn't come home until two o'clock last night. I asked her why she even bothers. You know what she said?"

"No." She noticed that the sorrel seemed to be holding his head higher and Maris thought his eyes looked clearer.

"She says she always comes home to me because I'm the one she loves. So I asked her why the hell she fucks around on me. She said I shouldn't get upset because it has nothing to do with me and I shouldn't take it personally. She implied that it's my fault if I let it affect our relationship. What do you think about that?"

"I think she'd try to sell ice trays in hell."

Shannon gave her a puzzled look and then a shy grin. "Yes, I guess she probably would." After rubbing her neck and stretching it tiredly, she said, "I saw in the paper where you found more bodies. Is it the same guy that sent you the note?"

"I think so. These murders may be related to two in Austin that occurred in 'eighty."

"I saw something in the paper about that."

"It was in the *Dallas Morning News* and the *Fort Worth Star Telegram* on the third. The *Austin Statesman* ran it on the second — the same day he set fire to my truck. I guess it could be a coincidence, but I tend to believe he saw or heard about the article and it triggered his actions. I also think he may have been the one who set off the alarm at the courthouse."

"If his goal in sending you the threatening note was to scare you away from investigating the Austin murders, the articles would have upset him." Shannon hopped off the fence.

"I don't know how he would have known about the Austin article unless he travels there for business regularly." Maris shrugged.

"By the way, what happened to your court case? I thought you'd come by the office yesterday."

"I guess we frightened the defendant; he pleaded guilty the next morning."

"He and his attorney must have seen the influence that you had with the jury."

Maris pretended to scowl at her. "I still think whoever called in the false alarm at the courthouse is the same person who sent me the package with the note and shoe and set fire to my truck."

"You may never know for sure. Did you see the baby in the second stall when you came in tonight?"

"Yes, how old is he? He looks unsteady on his feet still."

"He was born yesterday. I'm really excited about him. With his lineage, I expect big things from that little fellow." She opened the corral gate for Maris. "Let's put Buster in the stall and see how he does."

Maris helped Shannon give him another round of mineral oil and pain medication, and they continued to alternately rest and walk the sorrel. By three-thirty, he was drinking water eagerly and seemed more restful. He no longer tried to lie down and roll in his stall. By five, he'd quit pawing at the ground, but he occasionally stretched his back and looked at his side. This stopped after he was finally able to relieve his bowels. By six-thirty, his heart rate and temperature were normal.

"I believe the worst is over," Maris said.

"If we can keep him going until the antibiotics kick in, he might live another five years." Shannon smiled and leaned tiredly on the stall door. Her smile faded. "This may sound funny, but he's the only remaining link with my family. I'm not ready to lose him."

A loud clap of thunder sounded and they both jumped. Maris put her arm around Shannon. "It doesn't sound funny. He's been a part of your life for a long time." Maris's stomach growled and she realized she was starving. "He'll be okay for a while. Let me buy breakfast. How about a Denny's Grand Slam? On second thought, that may not be enough. Let's split an order of biscuits and gravy to go with it."

"And coffee. Lots of coffee."

Chapter Ten

The early morning sky was black to the west and thunder rumbled in the distance. They needed rain in Allen but radio reports indicated that most of Dallas and other counties to the east were out of luck. Shannon slumped against the corner of the pickup cab with her eyes closed. Exhaustion had gradually overcome her at breakfast. It should have taken only fifteen minutes to reach her house north of Aledo, a mile off of farm road 1187, but the rain slowed the rush-hour traffic to a crawl. Although it was getting lighter outside, the downpour obscured everything around them except for shadowy forms and the occasional blur of a passing vehicle. Maris made a left turn onto the caliche road that curved past Shannon's driveway. She could barely see the car that turned right off the same road and accelerated quickly away from the stop sign.

When she stopped in front of the barn, Maris shook Shannon's shoulder. She blinked and wiped her eyes. Glancing toward the house, she said, "Robin's still not home." Thunder boomed and BB-sized hailstones bounced off the truck. Shannon reached for the door handle as lightning lit up the barn. "This is like a spring thunderstorm. It's not supposed to do this in January. Looks like the wind blew the side door open." Pulling her coat up around her ears, she ran to the barn.

Maris decided to call Lauren before following Shannon. She hoped she could hear over the steady drum of raindrops hitting the truck. When the answering machine picked up, Maris turned off the phone, assuming Lauren had already left for work. As she reached for the door handle, Shannon startled her by banging on her window. She screamed something Maris couldn't understand and, with her fists clenched, she doubled over as if in agony. They were both soaked by the time Maris got her under the front eaves of the barn. She tried to get Shannon inside, but she balked.

"What happened?" Maris shouted. Shannon, crying uncontrollably, kept trying to sink to the ground. Grabbing her by both arms tightly, Maris pushed her into the barn.

Between sobs, Shannon said, "He's dead. Buster's dead. His throat . . ."

Maris left her hugging herself on the floor in the corner of the barn and ran to Buster's stall. She almost slipped on a thick pool of blood. The horse's muscular neck was slit from side to side. "Goddamn." She gasped, holding on to the top of the stall door. It must have taken tremendous strength and a razor-sharp instrument like a machete or Bowie knife to do that kind of damage. Buster was past needing help. She turned to take care of Shannon. A bloody shoe-print impression caught her eye. She dropped to her knee beside it, feeling sick. It was only a partial print, but she could tell it was made by a left Eagle Sniper/Commando boot with a deep cut on the third cross-shaped lug. His fucking Eagle boots. The son-of-a-bitch was like a goddamn shadow or ghost. He probably loved this weather. She paused at each stall to check the other horses.

Running back to Shannon, she pulled her up by the elbow and half carried her to the truck. She drove as close to her front door as possible, but before she'd let her leave the pickup, she pulled a leather zipper bag out from under the seat. She checked the load in her .38 S & W and stuck a brown leather clip-on holster in her waistband near the small of her back. The rain intensified as she waited for Shannon to unlock the front door. She made her wait on the bottom step of the staircase until she was satisfied that the first floor was secure. Holding Shannon around the waist, she felt her shiver against her side as she helped her up the stairs. Leaving her on the landing, Maris checked the second floor for intruders.

When she knew they were alone, she holstered the gun and said, "I'm sorry, Shannon. If I'd known anything like this could happen, I'd have never involved you in this case."

"It's not your fault." The tears started falling. "Poor Buster. What a horrible way to die." Shannon dropped to the side of the bed. "Oh, God." She went white, staring at Maris. "The baby," she whispered. "What about the baby?"

"He's fine. All of the other horses are fine. You need to get out of those wet clothes and into a hot shower before you catch pneumonia. Raise your foot and I'll help you get those wet boots off. While you're in the shower, I'll call the Tarrant County S.O."

"Parker, we're in Parker county," Shannon said as Maris pulled off her last boot.

They both jumped, like guilty lovers, when Robin said from the doorway, "What the fuck's going on here?"

"There's been some trouble. We were up all night —"

"I bet you were."

"Robin, please don't start anything," Shannon said, standing. She began to unbutton her flannel shirt.

Maris glared at Robin. "Shannon called me over to help with Buster."

"And you're just the one to help her."

Furious, Maris took a step forward.

"Maris," Shannon said. There was no inflection in her voice, no reproach, only tired resignation.

Maris stopped and forced herself to speak calmly. "He had colic but was better when we left for break-fast. When we got back, Shannon found him. He'd been killed — his throat cut."

"Jesus, who would do such a thing?" Robin's jaw dropped.

"A crazy motherfucker who's murdered at least seven women." Robin's sarcasm disappeared and she rushed to Shannon. Maris stepped aside. "It's probably the same bastard who tried to break in here earlier tonight while she was alone."

Shannon buried her head in Robin's shoulder. Robin held her tightly, making soothing sounds, apologizing. Maris could see Shannon's shoulders shaking as she cried.

In a low voice, she said, "Take care of her, Robin. I'll call the S.O. and see to things in the barn." Stopping at the door, she added, "I know you don't know what's going on, but you and Shannon may be in real danger. I think you should go somewhere for a few days. Shannon can explain later." Don't fuck this up, she almost added as she hurried down the stairs.

She called Parker county and asked for the sheriff. She'd known him for years and it would be better if she explained the situation to him directly. She heard the shower come on upstairs and suddenly felt aware of her own cold, wet clothes. Luckily, she had an extra pair of coveralls in the pickup. She missed Lauren and decided to call her as soon as she talked to the sheriff.

It was three o'clock in the afternoon when Maris opened the lab and dropped tiredly in her desk chair with a fresh cup of coffee. After she'd taken photographs of Buster and the bloody shoeprint impression, it had taken hours for her to clean the blood out of the barn. She was glad that the sheriff made arrangements for someone to take Buster away and that they were able to come immediately. Shannon's ranch manager, delayed by flooding near his house, arrived at eleven o'clock. He promised to stay on the premises while Shannon and Robin were gone and to watch the other horses.

She was having trouble understanding the motive for killing Buster. Before she left Shannon's, she'd gone around to the back door and found a muddy Eagle shoeprint on the porch. It was difficult for her to believe that this bastard would have been scared away from Shannon, if indeed she was his target, by one deputy. She thought he had purposely made enough noise at the back door for Shannon to hear him and call 911. He probably knew or guessed that they had processed the boot prints found near the bodies, so he made sure to leave a muddy shoeprint near the back door where they would find it. Maris bet that was all he planned to do originally, until he saw the sick horse and realized how much Buster meant to Shannon — and, after she arrived, how much Shannon meant to her. A chill had swept through her when she discovered that bastard had been watching them walk the horse. While cleaning up, she'd seen a dry spot outside a rear window in the barn. The roof overhang kept the area dry and the barn itself had blocked the wind. From there, the corral and Buster's stall were plainly visible. A pile of Marlboro cigarette butts told how long he'd waited. His determination and patience were disheartening. He would and could take this game, whatever it was, to any level. But why not Shannon instead of the horse? If he really wanted to hurt Maris, why not Shannon? After all, she'd been alone between the time the deputy left and Maris arrived.

Maris went into the kitchen for a second cup of coffee. She was exhausted. Maybe there was something about Shannon that didn't fit his victim profile — something that turned him off. But Jesus, what could that be? Her independence? Or maybe this was all part of the game? To make Maris wonder and guess. To keep her unsettled. Well, if so, it was working.

She was thinking about a shower and sleep when three of her biggest drug task forces arrived in rapid succession with a combined total of sixty drug cases including two marijuana submissions of over two hundred and fifty pounds each. After they left, she took two extra-strength aspirins and drank more coffee. She'd almost completed the paperwork when the evidence tech from Pierce County S.O. dropped in with the evidence taken from the body and skeletal remains.

Shortly after the tech left, Ralph faxed Maris an informal report announcing that all but one of the victims had been identified. He included brief victim profiles and a message from Wayne Coffey announcing the formation of a multi-agency task force to focus on the Pierce county rape-murders. The task force consisted of Wayne, Ralph, police department detectives from Dallas, Tyler, and Denton and an FBI agent from the Dallas office. Additional funding was also available for a temporary secretary and for laboratory assistance and analysis. A handwritten note asked Maris to join the task force as a forensic consultant, fees to be worked out later.

Pleased to be included, but somewhat surprised at how quickly the bodies were identified and the task force organized, Maris dropped into her desk chair to study the list of victims.

Ralph's list included Theresa Eastin, the first victim discovered. A legal secretary, she was twenty-three and lived in a condo in Dallas. She disappeared the Friday after Thanksgiving.

Katherine Galimore, twenty-five, was the most recent victim. She had disappeared on Christmas Eve from a parking garage near Mockingbird and Central Expressway in Dallas. She had been a real estate agent. Her body bore signs of torture similar to the injuries found on Theresa Eastin.

The partial skeleton, found farthest from the road, was identified as Phyllis Pierson, age twenty-four and a student at the University of North Texas in Denton. Authorities believed she disappeared from the UNT parking lot after attending a jazz concert in mid-October, nearly three months ago. She was reported missing by her roommate and parents.

The skeletal remains with strands of blonde hair nearby were identified as Jennifer Belton. At seventeen, she was the youngest victim. A high school student, she lived with her parents in Tyler. She had disappeared from in front of their home in mid-August.

One skeletonized body was still unidentified but believed to be a woman in her mid-twenties. Due to the condition of the remains, the medical examiner couldn't pinpoint the exact time of death. However, in keeping with the pattern established by the dates the other victims were abducted, he thought it conceivable that she had died in or around September.

This would mean, starting with Jennifer in August, one victim a month had been kidnaped and murdered.

Maris forced herself to finish her paperwork and log in all of the new drug cases. By the time she had the marijuana bricks stacked in the vault, it was almost six o'clock and she felt like she was at the end of her rope. Earnhardt was waiting for her, dancing to go outside. "Fellow, I'm so tired I could sleep leaning against a barbed wire fence," she said as she let him out. He barked as he rushed past her. Keeping a close eye on him from the kitchen window, she made a ham and cheese sandwich. When she heard Lauren come in the front door, she called Earnhardt inside and locked the door behind him. He dashed past her to greet Lauren.

"Guess what, lover?" Lauren asked, leaning against the kitchen bar as Earnhardt bounced his tennis ball across her feet.

"You're madly in love with me and couldn't wait to get home for a quickie before supper." Maris laughed, going to her for a kiss. Lauren tried to twist away, but Maris grabbed her around the waist and pulled her close, kissing her neck.

"Lover, I don't think you could stay awake for a quickie."

"You have no faith." Maris released her. "What's your news?"

"I'm on the task force to work the murders in Pierce county."

Maris stepped back, somewhat off balance, and gripped the bar.

"What's wrong?" Lauren asked. "I thought you'd be pleased."

"I don't want you on the task force."

Lauren's green eyes flashed angrily, but soon hurt replaced the anger. "Why not? I'm qualified to be there."

Maris paced into the living room and back. "Damn it, Lauren, why didn't you ask me first?"

"Is that it? Is that the problem? I didn't ask you first. Fuck you, I don't have to ask you anything."

She turned away and Maris grabbed her arm. "Goddamn it, don't walk away from me. You'd better talk to me when something you do affects both of us."

"Don't touch me. I'm staying on the task force. If you don't like it, you quit. I'm second in command, if I give the word, you'll be the one off the task force."

Maris released her arm. "That'd be a fucking mistake!" She whirled, walked to the back door and jerked it open. She remembered to unlock it but forgot about the safety chain at the top. So angry she was shaking, she yanked on the knob harder, breaking the chain.

Earnhardt squeezed past her legs and raced outside, but he kept his distance, watching her warily. Maris picked up a piece of firewood that he had gnawed on one end. With a grunt, she threw it as hard as she could. It slammed against the back fence, scattering paint chips. The last of her energy deserted her and she collapsed in a lawn chair. Earnhardt placed his head on her lap and she stroked his soft hair. "We can't take a chance on losing another girlfriend, can we, guy?"

The house was silent when they went inside. She thought Lauren was gone until she found her in the bedroom calmly packing an open suitcase. She stood in the doorway and watched until Lauren, sensing her presence, looked up from folding a sweater.

Maris sat on the bed. Lauren settled next to her and Maris put her arm around her. The fragrance of Lauren's perfume swept over her. She sighed. "Lauren, I'm sorry if I hurt your feelings. I know you're qualified to be on this task force, and, objectively, we need you. As your lover, I don't want you to have anything to do with it."

"We have to get past this. And this is the second time your temper has really scared me. I don't know what to do when you're like that."

"I'd never hurt you."

"Sometimes, I'm not so sure."

"I'm serious about not wanting you on the task force, but wait a minute, let me tell you why. This guy has keyed on me for some unknown reason. Obviously a different reason than he uses to choose his victims. I'm not anywhere close to fitting his victim profile . . . but you are."

"I know. That's the argument I used to convince my bureau chief to put me on the team."

"This guy is elusive and he's deliberate, sadistic . . ." Lauren stood and resumed her packing. "Damn it, you're not listening to me," Maris said, her voice rising.

"So, what are you saying? You don't want me on this task force because it's too dangerous?" She placed a hand on her hip and turned to face Maris.

"Yes."

"Are you sure that's the real reason? I think you don't want to share the excitement. And you damned sure don't want me to be in command. Control — that's what this is really about." Maris gritted her teeth. Without responding, she started out of the room. "Don't walk out on this. Say something," Lauren said in a strained voice.

"You've said enough for both of us," she called back without stopping.

She sat outside on the patio for a long time. There was a chill in the air, but it was still warm for January. They'd received less than a tenth of an inch of rain from the storms that flooded Tarrant county. Hungry, needing something to absorb the acid in her stomach, she returned to the kitchen and finished her sandwich. She didn't know where Lauren had gone, when she'd come home or if she was working on the case.

She almost dropped her glass of milk when she turned to find Lauren setting her keys and purse on the bar. "I couldn't leave town with this between us."

Maris smiled. "I'm glad you didn't. Where are you going?"

"I'm flying to Austin. I have an appointment to talk to Bill Rogers' ex-wife at nine o'clock tonight. Tomorrow I'm going to the lab to get the fingernail and copies of the case files from the nineteen eighty murders."

Maris took her hand and led her to the sofa. She sank into the corner near the armrest and pulled Lauren down next to her. "I'm glad you came back."

"We have to resolve some of this." Lauren brushed some dog hair off her pant leg and played with the crease. "I've always worked white-collar crime, and I'm not as familiar with violent cases as you are. But this is my job and I want to be part of the big cases as much as you do. If you're worried, then help me. You say you know this guy — tell me about him."

"I'm not a trained crime-scene profiler, but I've studied all of the material I can find about it. Not just *Mindhunter* by John Douglas, who retired from the FBI as head of the Investigative Support Unit, but —"

"I know who he is. I even heard him lecture once."

"Then you're familiar with some of these techniques. I've also read some of the original papers from the study funded by the Justice Department. Articles by Douglas, Ressler, Burgess and others in the *American Journal of Psychiatry*, *Behavioral Sciences and the Law*, even the *FBI Law Enforcement Bulletin*." She twisted on the sofa to face Lauren. "Some of this stuff is common sense and gut instinct. Lots of old detectives have it although they may not be able to express it as elegantly. You know I've always been fascinated by murder and what motivates the offender. I was about eight when I started reading the newspaper. I would follow high-publicity cases and try to figure out who did it and why. I'd listen to my dad and all of his police buddies. No one had ever heard of crime-scene profiling then or the psychology of the offender." She smiled somewhat embarrassed. "Sometimes I was right and sometimes I was wrong and, of course, I got better as I matured and came to understand more about life in general."

Lauren laughed. "You're admitting you're wrong. I can't believe it."

"I said I was wrong sometimes." Maris grinned.

"So tell me what you think about this guy."

"I'm telling you all of this because I want you to understand that this is not an exact science. It is a science and a powerful tool, but we don't know how often the profiles are wrong. Those offenders aren't caught and you don't write books about the ones who got away. These kinds of killers are like the stock market — past performance isn't always an accurate indicator of future performance. Sometimes he'll throw us curve balls when we expect split-fingered fast balls like this morning at Shannon's."

"I understand, and I still want to hear your ideas. It may be sometime before we can get an FBI profile."

Maris took a deep breath and looked down at her hands. "He's white, has a good job that allows him to travel the Dallas, Denton, Tyler triangle surrounding Pierce. He'll drive a vehicle with high mileage but in good condition, probably domestic. It may even be a model favored by law enforcement such as a Chevrolet Caprice. These guys like cops; some even want to be cops. They may imitate them, which probably explains why this guy wears Eagle boots. Or they may take jobs that bring them into contact with police. For example, a wrecker driver who tows vehicles damaged in traffic accidents for the highway patrol. Some seek out cop hangouts and they've been known to initiate conversations about their crimes. Age is tricky because, assuming he's also responsible for the nineteen eighty murders, he'll be older than we'd normally guess. Maybe thirty to forty or forty-five?" She shrugged. "I think he'll be an average-looking guy. Women won't fear him. Hell, the kind of women he likes probably won't even notice him. His vehicle might have modified locks and windows so escape is impossible. And I think he'll try to trick or lure his victims into his car rather than use brute force. He'll use whatever means is necessary for success." Maris squirmed on the sofa. "The autopsy reports indicate that Theresa Eastin and the most recent victim, Katherine Galimore, were held and tortured for several days before they were killed. They probably all were . . . except for the first two killed in 'eighty. I've thought about this. He was seventeen years younger then, possibly even a juvenile. I suspect he didn't have a good safe place to keep them then. He does now. A remote place, maybe soundproofed, equipped with restraints and torture devices — stun guns, whips, sharp knives. He's also had time to mature and refine his methods. The fantasies that drive him have evolved. He gets his pleasure from hurting them . . . until they're used up. But he'll try not to kill them too soon — even if he has to use basic first aid to keep them alive." She couldn't sit still any longer and walked to the fireplace where she leaned on the mantel. "I'm stuck on how he finds, stalks the women and, if they're all lesbians, how he knows this."

"I think you're afraid that I might have to be bait for him."

"I know you might have to be bait for him, but I'm worried that he already knows who you are and that we're lovers. After all, he connected Shannon to me and knew where to find her."

"Then I may already be in danger."

"Not as much as you will be if we really hang you out there. Dress you in the right way . . . make you easily available."

"We won't do that until we've exhausted every other option."

"So far we don't have anything else. He's proven to be unpredictable and clever." She returned to the sofa.

"If we have to use a woman to set a trap, maybe the woman from Tyler P.D. can do it. I might be needed in the surveillance van."

Maris raised her eyebrows and said, "Obviously you haven't met Sally Trent. She's about as likely to break her ankle in heels as I am."

Lauren pressed against her. "Are you saying she goes to our church?"

Relaxing, Maris said, "Does she ever. Sings in the choir."

"Good-looking?"

"Yeah, I'd say so, but she's not my type."

"That must make her my type then." Lauren was smiling, twirling a strand of hair.

Maris tried to scowl. "You're walking on thin ice there, girl." Gently, she touched her cheek and smoothed her red hair. "I'm sorry I lost my temper."

Lauren clutched her hand. "I know you're tired and upset about what happened this morning at Shannon's, but I think there may be something else going on here." Maris looked down at the floor. She knew the words before Lauren said them. "We're coming up on the anniversary of Mary Ann's death."

Maris shook her head negatively. "No, that's not it . . . at least, not all of it."

"I wish I didn't have to leave, but I'm running

late." Lauren retrieved her purse and keys from the kitchen. She paused. "We'll get through this."

Earnhardt whined at the door after she closed it. Maris understood how he felt. Why did she feel like they'd cut down a tire and were fixing to hit the wall at about a hundred and fifty miles per hour?

Chapter Eleven

It's amazing what ten hours of sleep can do for your attitude, Maris thought as she tackled the two large marijuana cases that came in the previous day. Up at five thirty, she had treated herself and Earnhardt to McDonald's sausage and biscuits for breakfast before opening the lab. It took her over three hours to weigh and sample each brick and clean the dust, loose marijuana and Carpetfresh out of the lab. She hated the fucking Carpetfresh they packed inside the plastic wrap in an effort to deter the dope dogs. It went everywhere, but at least it wasn't as messy as the bricks she'd seen with layers of mustard, ketchup or, Lord forbid, axle grease. By ten-thirty, she'd finished the microscopic examination of each sample and performed two different chemical tests for the identification of THC and other constituents of marijuana.

After typing her report, she poured a cup of coffee and sat down at her desk. She opened the envelope with the report and photographs Shannon had prepared from her examinations of the note. Shannon's letter documented a dozen partial telephone numbers and e-mail addresses. Most of the Internet addresses were either related to the news or sports as far as Maris could tell. Three telephone numbers seemed complete, two with a Dallas 214 area code. Maris dialed the first number. A sales clerk for a large computer store on Central Expressway answered. Maris requested the store's address and hours. A male answered the second number in three rings and said, "Gay and Lesbian Information Line, may I help you?"

Stunned, Maris slammed down the receiver. Why would this fucker be calling them, she wondered. The third number was an 800 line. When Maris tried it, she got a screeching noise. She supposed that it might be a fax line. She sipped her coffee, studying the photographs. She jumped when the telephone rang and grabbed it on the second ring. It took her a moment to recognize Kathy's voice. "It's over," she said. "Lynn moved out last night."

"I'm sorry to hear that."

"It was time, I guess. We made it two and a half years. I swear two years is my limit. From now on, I'm going to save myself some trouble and, at midnight of our second anniversary, out they go. Save myself the humiliation of getting dumped." Maris waited, letting her ramble. "Something's been wrong for a while. She finally broke down and told me she'd been fucking Valerie for three months."

"Valerie, as in Jan and Valerie?" Maris asked, thinking that was probably not the precise language Lynn used.

"I suppose it's Lynn and Valerie now. How do you do it, Maris? How did you get past the second anniversary?"

Maris laughed. "Don't ask me. I've only managed it once. I'm not sure Lauren and I will make it a year." She explained their argument over the task force.

"Is Lauren right? Are you being unfair?"

"Me, unfair? Never." Maris twirled a pen on her desk.

"Seems like I can remember a time or two when —"

"Okay, maybe I have been known to be unfair once in a great while."

"And selfish, don't forget selfish."

"Gee, thanks, Kathy. Now, I remember why I never tell you anything."

"You're welcome. But seriously, are you being unfair? After all, she is an FBI agent. She has her job to do like you have yours."

"I don't know. I understand the risk in police work. I wouldn't say a word about her working undercover narcotics. But this case is different. This guy is unpredictable, and he seems to be leaving a trail of destruction around me." Briefly, she told Kathy how he set fire to her truck and killed

Shannon's horse. "I can't explain how I feel, but I'm worried."

"If that's how it is, you better do everything you can to stay on the task force so you can be there if she needs you. That means keeping your concerns to yourself."

"Damn it, Kathy, I hate it when you're right."

"I'd think you'd be used to it by now. Come out with me tonight. We can grab a bite to eat and go dancing at the Midnight Sun. My next ex may be anxiously waiting for me there. You do remember how to dance, don't you?"

"Hell, yes, I remember how to dance, but no can do tonight. Maybe when this is over."

She'd just told Kathy good-bye when she was startled by a sharp rap on the glass door to the living room. She looked up to see Lauren. Wondering why she was so jumpy, she opened the door and said, "I didn't expect you back so soon."

After a kiss, Lauren held out a small box sealed with bright red evidence tape. "I have a present for you. The fingernail and a known blood sample from William Roy Hatcher. Also known samples from Allen and Keisler that were preserved frozen by the lab."

"Good, I was fixing to set up the samples from the medical examiner's office for DNA." She carried the samples to the desk and handed Lauren a submission form to fill out while she completed the records for the chain of custody.

"We got lucky," Lauren said as she wrote. "Wayne called from Houston and told me William Roy was visiting relatives in Austin. I tracked him down. I expected him to give me a hard time, but he volunteered a sample. He told me that he'd told Detective

Wheeler — senior — a couple of years ago that he'd submit to DNA testing. I called little Al and he told me he read in his father's journals that his dad thought Hatcher was innocent. Unfortunately, the notes were unclear about what evidence he had."

"What about Bill Rogers?"

"His ex-wife wasn't much help. She doesn't keep up with him. She did tell me that he made bizarre sexual demands on her while they were married. But she wouldn't go into details so I don't know what she considers bizarre. She also said their marriage was already rocky, but it deteriorated rapidly after the murders." She signed the papers where Maris indicated. "I have to go, lover. Can you meet me at three-thirty for a task force organizational meeting?" She tore off a yellow Post-it note and jotted down an address. "This is our new office in Rockwall that Ralph leased. He thought it would be a convenient location for the Dallas, Denton and Pierce county officers. Sally Trent will have the longest drive. I'm looking forward to meeting her."

"Just remember whose closet your shoes are in, girl," Maris teased as Lauren left.

She'd already cut the seal on the box and removed the small coin envelope with the fingernail. Since a fingernail consists of a hard keratinous material, she had to boil it for five minutes in distilled water to soften it. When the timer went off, she used a sterile scalpel to shave away thin slivers of it and then placed them in a buffer to soak overnight. She glanced at the clock and saw that it wasn't yet noon. With luck and no interruptions, she could get through the samples from the M.E.'s office before the task force meeting and collect what she needed for DNA typing.

She started with the evidence from Katherine Galimore's body. She broke the seal on the green and white box labeled Sexual Assault Kit and inventoried the items. The medical examiner had taken vaginal, oral and rectal samples that were submitted as smears on air-dried slides and on cotton swabs. The kit also contained pubic hair combings and known head hair and pubic hair from the victim. Galimore's kit was all she had to work with, since no sexual assault evidence was collected from the other victims due to the condition of the remains.

Maris was hopeful that enough sperm could be detected for DNA typing. Sperm had been discovered in deceased victims for one to two weeks after death even though the decomposition of the body starts immediately and can affect the biological evidence of sexual assault. It was the medical examiner's opinion that the body had been cleaned before it was dumped. But as in the samples taken from Theresa Eastin's body, he located sperm in the cervical samples, and Maris thought there were enough present on the slide for DNA.

She found no foreign hair in the pubic hair combings and turned her attention to the clothing removed from the body. At least they'd air-dried the clothes at the M.E.'s office, therefore making the odor bearable. She collected several white cotton fibers from the green dress, similar to those that she'd removed from Theresa's clothing. She suspected both victims had been wrapped in a white sheet. She stopped work in time to grab a sandwich before the task force meeting. If it was short enough, she would start her DNA extractions when she returned.

Maris arrived early, but the new task force office already contained a stream of ant-like activity. Viola Smith, a secretary retired from DPS, greeted her with a hug. Five computers and printers were scattered around the room, some new and some loaned by member police agencies. Most of the officers were working to hook up phone lines, computers and fax machines, and to hang bulletin boards. A refrigerator and coffee machine were already in place.

Sally Trent, in blue jeans and a flannel shirt, rose from the floor where she was running computer cable. A swimmer in college, she was tall, thin and lanky with small breasts. She brushed her sandy bangs away from her forehead and shook Maris's hand. Dusting her knees, she said, "It's good to see you. I've missed you at DPS. We're hurrying to get these computers ready. Lauren has some FBI whiz coming by later to network them and get our software loaded and the word processors up and running." Lauren, returning from the back storeroom, waved at Maris. Sally lowered her voice and said, "She told me you weren't happy about her being on the task force."

"She shouldn't have said anything."

"I understand why you're upset."

"I never wanted a girlfriend in law enforcement, but . . ." She shrugged.

Sally squeezed Maris's shoulder and winked. "Hell,

just a girlfriend would be nice." She returned to her task.

Maris watched Wayne, Ralph and Lauren at a table in the back of the room. Lauren, consulting her notes, pinned crime scene photographs on a brown corkboard on the table.

Wayne said, knocking on the table for attention, "I know the room is crowded, but please find a seat somewhere and let's get started. Help yourself to coffee or soft drinks." After everyone was in place, he continued, "At this time, the task force consists of myself; Ralph Lambert, Pierce County Chief Deputy; Lauren O'Conner, FBI; Sally Trent, Tyler P.D.; Daniel Westmoreland, Dallas P.D.; Jeff Bell, Denton P.D.; Maris Middleton, Middleton Forensic Services; and Viola Smith, our task force secretary. Albert Wheeler of Austin P.D. will be joining us in a day or two. We are funded fifty, twenty-five, twenty-five percent with respectively, federal, state, and a combination of funds from each of your police departments."

He paused to read his notes and Maris used the opportunity to study the faces in the room. She smiled at Daniel Westmoreland, the only one she didn't know, and he nodded. Daniel was a tall, muscular black man with a sharply trimmed mustache and goatee, elegantly dressed in an expensive suit and a light blue shirt with a flashy tie. She turned her attention back to Wayne.

"Although most of the money is federal, this is a local case that will be tried in state district court. So it was decided that I'd be the task force commander. Lauren is second in command. She and I will coordinate the investigation and assign duties. We can thank Ralph Lambert for getting the task force paperwork together so quickly, finding this office space and rounding up the computers and office equipment for us. Some overtime money is available, but not much. I expect we'll cheat and work a lot more hours than we get paid for."

Everyone laughed. Ralph passed out a roster of names, addresses and telephone numbers for each member of the task force.

Lauren stood and said, "This is what we have so far. We have five dead bodies, but one skeleton has yet to be identified. The four identified are all white females."

Wayne pinned a map to the wall with markers in red indicating where the bodies were found while Ralph passed out information listing each victim by name and age as well as describing her occupation and the place and time she disappeared.

Lauren said, "I'll let Maris tell you about shoe-print and other scientific evidence."

Maris pushed her chair back and stood. "The shoeprints left near the bodies were made by Eagle Sniper/Commando Special boots that were favored almost exclusively by police SWAT teams, outdoorsmen, militia types, skinheads and neo-Nazis until recently. Now, they're popular footwear for nearly everyone. The shoes are sold in only two stores in Texas but can be ordered by mail. Sperm were detected on cervical slides taken during autopsies on Theresa Eastin and Katherine Galimore. There is enough for DNA typing, but there's a hazard to using cervical samples. Spermatozoa tend to survive longer in this tissue and could be there from a consensual sexual partner before the assault, although this is unlikely in this case because of the length of time he holds his victims before they're killed. Also, we think he attempts to clean them before dumping the bodies. That and the advanced state of decomposition explain why no seminal fluid was detected in the vaginal vaults. Guys, this bastard knows a lot about forensic evidence. I attended Theresa Eastin's autopsy. It looked to me like he washed and combed her hair, including the pubic area, to remove any hair he may have inadvertently transferred. White cotton fibers were detected on both Theresa's and Katherine's clothing, indicating they were probably wrapped in white sheets."

Lauren smiled at her warmly, igniting a fire in her chest. She dropped into her chair and Lauren said, "On December twenty-seventh, Maris received a threatening note and one black Lovelady brand right shoe in a box delivered by UPS. The shoe led us to two murders that occurred in Austin in March and April of nineteen eighty. We believe these murders are related to ours, but don't know if it's the same killer or a copycat with intimate information about the first two murders, perhaps someone close to the original investigations." Lauren paused as Ralph passed the 1980 photographs of Cynthia Allen and Debbie Keisler around the room. "State Senator W. R. Hatcher's son, William Roy, was the prime suspect. No seminal fluid or foreign blood was found on either victim. A broken fingernail was found in the second victim's hair, but DNA typing wasn't available then. Yesterday, I went to Austin and got the fingernail from the lab. I also obtained a blood sample from Hatcher. Maris now has these items."

"Rushing the lab already?" Maris grinned. "If

everything works, I should have the results on the fingernails, sperm samples and William Roy's blood in two days."

Lauren gestured to the Ranger. "Wayne went to Houston to check up on Hatcher. After checking the dates of the victims' disappearances with his activities, we think the DNA will clear him — at least in our murder investigations."

"One more thing," Maris added. "Barbara Shelton, the DPS serologist in 'eighty who investigated the Austin murders, told me a partial shoeprint was observed near one of the bodies. Unfortunately, it was destroyed accidentally before examination-quality photographs or casts could be made. I showed her one of the casts I made of the Eagle boot sole pattern, and she thinks the shoeprint she saw in 'eighty could have been similar."

"It's not likely the man is still wearing the same shoes after seventeen years," Jeff Bell said, looking up from his notes.

"No, but I've been told the wearers of these boots are very brand-loyal. The style of the boot and the sole tread pattern haven't changed since inception, twenty-five years ago. I agree it's a stretch, but our killer might simply like these boots."

Wayne interrupted. "We're trying to get a court order for catalogue records of sales made in north Texas in the last two years and Austin in 'seventy-nine and 'eighty. If there's a name common to both lists, maybe we'll have a suspect."

"Good." Lauren nodded. "Let's discuss the victims. All of them were abducted from the Dallas area except for one. Jennifer Belton, our youngest victim, disappeared within a block of her home in Tyler. We're studying the break in pattern." Lauren paused and took another sip of water. She glanced in Maris's direction and Maris knew what was next. Lauren cleared her throat and said, "Both the north Texas and Austin victims had long fingernails painted in a shade of red and wore black high-heeled shoes. We even found the remains of red artificial sculptured nails — also called acrylic tips — on the ground around our unidentified skeletal remains. We believe that the victims may have one other trait in common. I hesitate to mention it since it hasn't been confirmed for all of them yet. This information can have devastating effects on the families and friends of the dead women, but it's too important to ignore. We think all of the victims were lesbians."

Maris didn't react, but Sally, unprepared, squirmed in her seat. Maris glanced down at the task force roster where the common address and phone number for her and Lauren seemed to be a red flag. She smiled wryly at Sally.

Whispering in Maris's ear, Sally said, "So much for worrying about the source of cervical sperm samples."

Maris nodded as Lauren continued. "For the first assignments, Wayne and I have determined that these avenues should be investigated first. We'll welcome any suggestions, but for now, Sally and I will work on the victim profiles. Are they all lesbians, and if so, how did our killer know this? Ralph and Albert will get the search warrant for the catalogue sales of

Eagle boots and investigate the customers on the list. I've got an FBI computer expert lined up to help them narrow the number of likely suspects using an offender profile we're building. Also I traced the UPS package Maris received to the Mail Shoppe in Tyler. Wayne contacted the manager, but she won't release her records without a court order. Jeff, I want you to handle that." She nodded to the Denton P.D. detective. "I'm making a list of sex offenders who've been in prison from April, nineteen eighty until this last July or August and reside in our area." She glanced at her notes. "We suspect Theresa Eastin's body was dumped in a separate place because a road crew was working on the highway near the other bodies and the murderer couldn't get to his favorite location. Detective Westmoreland will interview the road crew and find out if they can describe the man or his vehicle. Jeff Bell will also research the earliest information on each woman's disappearance and talk to any witnesses who may have seen them last. Some of this has been done before, but let's do it again in case something was missed the first time." Lauren paused. "To close, we don't have an official FBI profile of this murderer yet. Wayne and Ralph will complete the VICAP report as soon as possible. For anyone who doesn't know what this is, it is a detailed crime analysis report that's sent to the Violent Criminal Apprehension Program in the National Center for the Analysis of Violent Crime at the FBI Academy. Once completed, I'll go over it with the criminal-profile coordinator in the Dallas field division, and it'll be sent to the FBI Investigative Support Unit. The profile might help us identify a potential suspect and interrogate him when he's caught. Does anyone have anything else?"

Maris raised her hand. "From the photograph Ralph has, Jennifer Belton was pretty with blond hair. Wayne, you're probably thinking what I am." For the benefit of the other officers in the room, she added, "Last September when we were looking for Lauren's niece, her boyfriend, Brian Blake, became a prime suspect in her disappearance and was ultimately proven to be involved. During the investigation, the Blakes' foster kid reported sexual abuse to a school counselor and gave information that she had observed a blonde teenage girl in captivity at the Blake house. She said the girl was repeatedly raped and tortured. Long shot, but maybe we should see if she can identify Jennifer as that girl."

"I agree, Maris," Wayne said. "We never found evidence that the blonde teenager existed except for the kid's story. But she was convincing. I'll handle it."

Lauren said, "We've talked very little about suspects other than Hatcher. But there are two other men associated with the first two murders in Austin that we want checked out. Debbie Keisler's husband and the DPS photographer, Bill Rogers. Wayne searched for Mr. Rogers in Houston but couldn't find him. We have information that he resigned from DPS under a cloud after two women claimed he assaulted them during private photography sessions. Witnesses claim he was deeply affected by the murders. What else, Wayne?"

He stood and she sat on the edge of her chair. "The medical examiner is ready to release the remains of the victims. I want at least one of us at each funeral. I'll make assignments later. We have a toll free number that we'll publicize on posters and in the newspapers soliciting information from the public, and we'll soon have a Web page on the Internet. Viola will be here from eight to five everyday to help with the phone lines and do our bookkeeping and typing. I'd like one of us to be here with her to take phone calls and follow up on any new information, but I realize that may not always be possible. Does anyone have anything to add?"

"Yes," Maris said. "I think everyone should know what else this bastard has done." She described how he set fire to her truck and killed Shannon's horse. She also explained the questioned-document work that Shannon did on the note and what was found.

"What about your safety?" Daniel asked.

"I'm not in any danger. If he wanted to kill me, he could have already. The women around me may be in danger, but I'm not." She started to add how worried she was about Lauren's safety but didn't after remembering Kathy's advice.

Jeff Bell twirled his pen between his fingers and said, "From the e-mail addresses and the phone number to the computer warehouse, it sounds like our guy might be a computer nerd."

"Maybe," Maris said, "but there's no way to know if it's a business or a hobby."

"Either way, he might have met the women on-line — in a chat room."

Ralph ran his fingers through his mustache. "If so, maybe someone will call us or e-mail us when our computers are up. Someone else is going to have to handle this. This cowboy don't know shit about e-mail. But that's a good idea, Jeff. Maybe you can look into it?"

The meeting broke up and Maris glanced at her watch. It wasn't even five o'clock yet — not that it mattered. Forty-hour work weeks and overtime for more ended the day she quit DPS. If she hurried home, she could start extracting her samples in preparation for DNA typing.

Chapter Twelve

A choking sound and muffled scream startled Maris out of a deep sleep. The bed shook, and Maris sat up searching the room for an intruder until she realized that Lauren was grappling with an invisible opponent and attempting to reach the gun usually holstered behind her back.

"Lauren, honey, wake up!" Maris said, shaking her shoulder gently.

"No, no!" she yelled, lashing out with her hands.

Maris ducked. "Wake up! It's only a dream. You're fine."

Panting, she abruptly stopped struggling and sat up. Maris snapped on the nightstand lamp and threw her arms around her.

"It's okay, honey. It's only a dream." She stroked her hair, rocking gently back and forth. Earnhardt leapt on the bed beside Lauren and licked her face. "See, Earnhardt's worried about you."

She laughed shakily, petting the dog. Satisfied she was okay, he jumped down. "Oh, God, it was so real." Although she wore a nightshirt with long sleeves, she shivered.

Drawing her close, Maris asked, "Do you want to tell me about it?"

"What a nightmare! A man approached me in the office parking lot to ask directions. Before I knew what happened, I was in handcuffs locked in the backseat of his car with no door handles, no way to unlock it. He took me to an old house and chained me in the basement. He started to do things to me . . ." She closed her eyes and swallowed hard. "Turn off the light and hold me."

When the room was dark except for a shaft of light that filtered through the crack in the curtains, Maris slid down in the bed and hugged her. Soft hair tickled her cheek, and she could feel the warmth of Lauren's breath against her bare chest.

"Your profile of the killer, is it accurate, or were you trying to scare me?" Lauren asked.

"Both, and it should scare you. It scares the hell out of me."

"We have to find out how he's targeting these women, how he finds them and how he knows they're lesbians. Soon." Lauren shuddered.

"One of us — you, Sally or me will figure it out," Maris said.

"So I'm on the team?"

"Damn it, Lauren. It's not funny. I still wish you weren't on the task force."

"I'm not trying to be funny. This isn't going to break us up, is it?"

"Not a chance." She kissed her forehead and sighed. "I've been thinking. If I were the killer, I'd haunt the women's bars — take them off of the parking lot as they leave. Lord knows the security sucks at most of them."

"But we know that's not how he did it. He knows where they work, go to school. Where they live. How?" Lauren drew a deep breath. "Could he be dressing as a butch . . . to attract the femmes?"

"I doubt it. It took a lot of power to cut Buster's throat. I don't think he could or would want to pass as a woman. He'd consider it beneath him."

They lay quietly and Maris felt Lauren gradually relax until she was sleeping peacefully. Her shoulder and arm went numb, but she didn't want to disturb Lauren. How many lives has this guy fucked up, she wondered. Not just the loss of life but the pain and suffering of the families, friends and lovers of each victim. The investigators whose lives were touched. They could be looking for this guy for months, maybe years, and it'd already caused a rift between her and Lauren. God, what if he was like the Green River killer and never caught?

Pain forced her to shift slightly. Lauren moaned

but didn't wake. Maris smiled; she was so beautiful and smart and fun. Exciting. How could she take a chance on losing her? Maris was wide awake now — her mind racing. If she was a white male with a thing for lesbians, how would she find them? That used to be a problem she and Toni had in college. When they could scrape up the money, they'd go to Dallas, Austin or Houston. If they didn't know where to find the women's bars, they'd call the Gay Hotline. It was almost always staffed by some queen, but he could usually find them an acceptable bar, at least for a start, with a bartender who could direct them to the right bar. Not that it did them any damn good. But they always started out with such courage and high hopes.

So, assuming he found the bars and the woman he wanted, what then? They weren't taken from the bar parking lots or side streets. Somehow, he knew the addresses, occupations, even schools of his victims. Who would a woman going to or from a gay bar give her address to voluntarily? Another woman? On rare occasions, these guys were known to use a woman to help procure their victims. But more often they worked alone. She almost dozed when it hit her. A police officer! She forgot about Lauren on her shoulder and tried to sit up.

"What's wrong?" Lauren asked sleepily, rolling over onto her side.

"I know how he tracks down his victims."

"What?" Lauren sat upright.

"I know how he gets their addresses. Shannon found the phone number for the Gay and Lesbian Information Line in Dallas in the indentations on the note. I think he called, made up some story about a lesbian friend and requested the addresses for the women's bars. He's police or has a police uniform. If someone sees him hanging around, they assume it's his assigned beat or he's off duty security hired by the bar. When a woman leaves that he's interested in, he follows her. He drives a police type vehicle probably equipped with blue and red lights. He stops her for speeding, running a stop sign, driving erratically, whatever, and asks for her driver's license. Instead of a citation, he writes her a warning ticket requiring all the pertinent information such as address, occupation and telephone number and keeps a carbon copy."

"We thought about a cop. It's happened before, but there are no reports of any unusual police activity or complaints about police behavior. No indications of an imposter."

"There wouldn't be, because none of the women will complain. They're relieved to get off with a warning, especially if they've been drinking. He's probably polite, doing nothing unusual to arouse their suspicions. They believe it's a righteous stop. Hell, he could be a real cop."

"Who would stop for an unmarked police car late at night?"

"Most women, especially if they've been drinking. The ones who are suspicious and try to drive to a police station or the fire station on Cedar Springs, he simply lets go. All he has to do is turn down a side street with lights flashing. She'll assume he had another call and wasn't after her at all. She'll laugh at herself for being paranoid, go home and forget about it."

"Oh God, Maris, you could be right. When he's

ready, he watches his victim's home or business. If she's not dressed like he wants or something turns him off, he goes to another address on his list. Sooner or later, he'll find a professional woman who dresses to suit him. Jesus, he wouldn't have to do this very often. He could work the bars for a couple of weekends and get lots of addresses. Save them until he needs them."

"We found a speeding ticket in Cynthia Allen's purse. Barbara Shelton told me she got the ticket on her way home from the bar two days before she was killed."

"Tomorrow, when Sally and I interview the people who knew the victims, we'll try to find out if any of the women received a warning ticket before they disappeared. This could be our big break. I'm too excited to sleep. How about you?" Lauren reached for Maris. "You interested?"

"Am I a-living and a-breathing?" she asked, falling into Lauren's arms.

Chapter Thirteen

On Saturday morning, her hair still damp from the shower, Maris locked the front door and rushed down the driveway to the black 1997 Pontiac Firebird. The Firebird was a confiscated vehicle released for government use and assigned to Lauren. Maris was dying to take her for a spin but hadn't managed to talk Lauren into it.

"Get a good workout?" Lauren asked as Maris slid into the passenger seat.

"Yes, while I ran my DQ-alphas." At Lauren's

puzzled expression, she added, "DNA typing. I read the results before I took my shower."

"Any results you can give me yet?"

"William Roy Hatcher is eliminated as the sperm donor in the Eastin and Galimore cases and as the source for the fingernail. But the samples are all from the same guy — just not Hatcher. I'll run D1S80s tomorrow. It's another system that'll make the results more specific when we get a suspect."

"It takes a long time to get DNA results, doesn't it?"

"It takes at least fifteen hours — assuming everything works the first time and there are no interruptions. Two full working days is about as soon as you'll hear anything back on DNA. Add an extra day for a fingernail or hair sample that has to be soaked overnight."

"I'm glad it worked out where you could come." Lauren glanced her way. "You look nice."

"I'm just wearing what I always do." She wore black starched and pressed Wranglers, a white long-sleeved shirt and a gray Western-cut jacket with her black eel belt and matching boots. "You look better than nice." She smiled appreciatively. Lauren wore brown slacks with a matching jacket and a beige low-cut blouse with heels. "Too bad we have to go to a funeral."

"Yes, especially to bury a teenager. With Katherine Galimore's and Phyllis Pierson's yesterday and Jennifer Belton's today, it's been a somber two days. I didn't think Sally and I would ever get back from Wichita Falls last night."

"At least with the funeral on Saturday, her friends won't miss any school."

"When I was in the fifth grade, a girl in our class was kidnapped on the way home. Two or three days later, they found her dead. It was horrible — I'll never forget it." Lauren tightened her grip on the steering wheel. "It could have been any one of us. Why her? Why not me or another girl? My grandmother took me to the funeral. The church was packed. Since I've been with the FBI, I've wondered if he was there."

"Did they catch him?"

"Never. Someday I'd like to reopen that case." Lauren shrugged. "Not that it would do any good."

"Yesterday was a long one for me too. I spent nearly sixteen hours in the lab. I thought you'd wake me up last night when you came home."

"You were sleeping so soundly and looked so cute, I didn't want to disturb you."

"We're probably both better rested today because you didn't." Maris stretched in her seat. "What's going on with the task force?"

"Jeff Bell is working the phones since Ralph is flying to Virginia to serve the warrant on the Eagle boot catalogue company. Daniel spent yesterday interviewing the road crew. He had to find an interpreter to help. The crew says that they saw a man pull over to the side of the road in a late model white Ford Crown Victoria but didn't get the license plate number. One man saw the suspect's face from a distance of about ten feet. They put together a composite drawing. I have a copy with me."

"Maybe things will start falling into place soon." Maris looked out the window of the Firebird. "It's dry around here. Too bad they didn't get the rain Fort Worth did."

"Yes, we need a good rain," Lauren said absently. "Sally and I talked to Katherine Galimore's lover and some of her friends yesterday. It's so sad. Katherine's family is trying to take everything. Her lover inherited the condo outright, but it looks like she'll lose the car and furniture. She may even lose the Sheltie they raised from a puppy."

"There'd be another killing before they got my dog. I didn't have any problems with Mary Ann's family, but we had a will."

"Katherine's favorite bar was the Midnight Sun in Dallas."

"It's a nice bar, plays mostly country music. You'd like it. It's between Cedar Springs and Lemmon on Throckmorton."

"One of Katherine's friends was with her when she received a warning ticket from a Dallas police officer two weeks before she disappeared."

"That's two of our victims that we know received a ticket, Cynthia Allen in Austin and now Katherine Galimore."

"Three, add Phyllis Pierson to your list. Her roommate was very reluctant to admit they were lovers. Phyllis's parents don't know, and her lover doesn't want them to find out. When this case breaks, it's going to have some devastating effects. We're going to inadvertently out a lot of women."

"I know."

"Phyllis's lover finally talked to Sally. She remembers that Phyllis received a warning ticket for running a stop sign after they left the Midnight Sun. I've got Daniel checking Dallas P.D. records."

They flew around three tractor trailer trucks before Lauren dropped the Firebird back into the right-hand lane. Maris jumped when her beeper, set to vibrate, went off. Lauren handed her the telephone and she dialed the number on the pager. "This is Barbara Shelton. I read about the task force in the paper. I can't believe they got organized so fast. Is it true that you have a blood sample from Hatcher and the fingernail to do DNA?"

"That's true."

Barbara sighed. "I heard that they think DNA will eliminate Hatcher."

"I can't say any more, Barbara."

"Damn it, Maris, I've been working these cases longer than you have. I have a right to know what's going on."

"Then you know that I will only release information to the lead investigators on these cases. Hell, on any case. I only admitted that I have the fingernail because you analyzed the original evidence. And I understand how you feel. I'd feel the same way —"

"Don't patronize me. You can't possibly know how I feel —" Maris thought she heard a sob escape Barbara. She was about to tell her she had to go when Barbara said, "I'm sorry. Forgive me, I'm way out of line here. Everything that I thought I'd forgotten has been bubbling to the surface the last few days. I've hated Hatcher for so long. If it's not him, I want to know who the fuck it is."

"I'll tell you what I can, but no promises." Feeling guilty, Maris turned off the phone and set it on the console.

Lauren said, "I thought you'd tell her. In some ways she has a right to know."

"I won't tell her anything. At least, not until you and Wayne and I have discussed it. I'm almost afraid to tell her the results. What if she does something foolish?"

"Like what?"

"I don't know." Maris shook her head. "If we decide to release the information to the press, I want to tell her first."

"I think that's only fair. Want to stop for a cup of coffee? We have time."

"Sure," Maris said, thinking she'd rather have a shot and a beer. God, how she hated funerals.

The expansive sanctuary of the First Baptist church in downtown Tyler was empty when Maris and Lauren entered an hour before the funeral, although many of the mourners loitered in the hallways and the parking lot, speaking in low voices. An earnest young man greeted them politely and, to Maris's surprise, introduced himself as the pastor.

"We don't want to be a distraction," Lauren said after showing her ID. "But we like to observe the people who attend funerals in cases like this."

"Yes, I've heard that," the pastor said. "You're more than welcome, and if there's anything I can do, don't hesitate to ask. Excuse me, I have to prepare for the services."

A few minutes later a man and woman beckoned to them from the back of the church. "I'm William Belton and this is my wife, Karen," the thin, sandy-haired man said.

"Come on back," Karen Belton said. "We have coffee and Cokes. It'll be a while before the service."

"We don't want to impose on you and your

family," Maris said, surprised to see that Mr. and Mrs. Belton were young, probably only five years older than she was.

"We long ago accepted the fact that Jennifer was gone, taken from us. It's a relief to have her back for proper burial," Mr. Belton said, holding the door open.

Mrs. Belton added, "Please come back and talk to us. We have no idea what is going on with the investigation. We didn't know they had formed a task force until we read about it in the paper."

"I'm sorry, ma'am," Lauren said. "We're still getting organized. I'll see to it that we formulate a plan to keep the family members informed of our progress."

They followed the Beltons into a community room and sat at a small table where Mrs. Belton insisted on serving them coffee. "Could you tell us about Jennifer? What she was like? Who her friends were?" Lauren asked.

Mr. Belton beamed. "She was a wonderful daughter. Never caused us any problems. She made good grades and was an all-state basketball player. She had hoped to go to Texas Tech or UT on a basketball scholarship, although Tennessee expressed an interest. She'd have been a senior this year." He momentarily looked away.

Mrs. Belton held his hand and continued for him. "Her boyfriend was Cody Hoffmeir. We worried that she was getting too serious about him, but she said that he was her best friend, after Tracy Roper. She and Cody with Tracy and her boyfriend, Jason Grant, went everywhere together. I miss having them hang out at the house. We asked Cody to sit with the family, but he wanted to sit with the other kids."

"The basketball team dedicated the season to Jennifer. I heard Tracy has several scholarship offers although she'll probably go to the University of Texas," Mr. Belton said, looking down at his coffee cup. "To think she disappeared from her own front yard."

Lauren reached over and touched his hand. "Thank you, Mr. and Mrs. Belton, for talking to us. We're sorry for your loss, and we'll do everything we can to find whoever is responsible."

Returning to the sanctuary, they saw the bronze casket, surrounded in a sea of roses and carnations, centered in front of the pulpit. An orange floral basketball draped in ribbons of the high school colors decorated the casket and blunted the harsh glare of the bronze. To Maris, it animated the short life of a dead teenager and brought reality to the loss. They stopped near the casket to study a half-dozen carefully arranged photographs of Jennifer, smiling and laughing. In two photographs, an equally pretty brunette accompanied her. In one picture, Jennifer, two handsome boys and the brunette, all with damp hair and dripping swimsuits, sprawled haphazardly across the bow of a flashy red-and-white ski boat.

"She was beautiful, intelligent and athletic," Maris whispered, touching the cold surface of the casket. "Everything a woman should be whether she's someone's daughter, sister, mother or lover. We can't afford to keep losing women like this."

"It's . . . more than a tragedy," Lauren said in a strained voice. They made their way to the back corner pew and watched as the rest of the church quickly filled. "Maris, does Jennifer fit our victim profile?"

"What do you think?" Maris said, nodding toward two slender young men entering the sanctuary, one on each side of a sorrowful dark-haired young woman. It was easy to recognize them from the photographs.

"They're all gay, covering for each other," Lauren whispered. "It'll kill Jennifer's parents when they find out. These kids are too young to have to deal with coming out publicly."

"Maybe they won't have too. We need to talk to them . . . find out if they've been to a gay bar and if Jennifer received a traffic ticket. After that, we can leave it alone."

"It'll come out when we catch this guy, especially during the trial."

"We'll see. Lord, can you imagine losing your lover at seventeen? It's hard enough at thirty-one."

Maris squeezed Lauren's hand and slipped out midway through the service to photograph the vehicles in and around the church, paying special attention to Chevrolet Caprices and Ford Crown Victorias. After the service, as unobtrusively as possible, she videotaped the crowd leaving the church. It was cool enough for a light jacket, but the January sun felt warm. Thinking of Jennifer's family, Maris was glad it was not raining. While they lined the cars up for the trip to the grave site, Lauren and Maris scrutinized the male mourners, especially those thirty to forty-five years old. At the cemetery, Lauren joined the graveside services while Maris stayed in the vehicle to discreetly run the video recorder.

Returning to the Firebird, Lauren said, "The kids have agreed to meet us at a restaurant nearby, The Ranchhouse. I have directions."

The three teenagers were already seated in a spacious booth in the rear of the steakhouse when Lauren and Maris arrived. "They look like they expect an inquisition," Maris said under her breath as they approached the table. All three sat on one side of the table leaving the other side for Lauren and Maris. The brunette sat between the two boys.

Maris waited for Lauren to slide in first and Tracy caught her eyes with a short-lived ripple of understanding. Lauren introduced herself and Maris. Cody, the stockier of the two men, spoke for the group. Maris detected a subtle, delicate effeminacy in his mannerism. Jason, on the other hand, acknowledged them much more flamboyantly.

"This isn't going to be easy," Lauren said. "We have to ask you some things you won't want to answer, but it's important in finding Jennifer's killer."

"Did she suffer?" Tracy asked in a low voice, barely audible over the din of clanging dishes.

Maris hesitated. "We don't know exactly how she died." She hoped this answer would suffice. She wasn't going to tell this senior in high school that her young lover suffered horrible, painful indignities and was brutally raped and mutilated. She would hear the truth soon enough if there was a trial.

The conversation paused as the waitress took orders and returned with iced tea for Lauren and Maris. The boys drank soft drinks and Tracy drank black coffee.

"Were you lovers?" Lauren asked.

Tracy looked at Cody and then back at Jason. "Is

this necessary?" Cody asked. "Everyone knows she's my girlfriend. We've dated since the eighth grade."

"It's important, Cody. We think the murderer was targeting lesbians."

"Yes, we were lovers," Tracy said in a low voice. "We wanted to go to college together, to live together." She looked straight at Maris and added, "You understand?"

"Yes, I understand. Did you ever go to a gay bar?"

This question brought a smile from the boys and a slight upper turn to the corner of Tracy's mouth. "Almost every Saturday night," she said. "On our double date."

"Which bar?"

"Usually the one in Longview. Occasionally, when we had money, we'd sneak off to Dallas, to the Crossroads. Sometimes we'd drop the boys off at a men's bar and come back for them later."

"How did you get in?"

Again the three exchanged glances. Jason said, "We tried to dress older, and we have fake ID's."

Maris continued to ask the questions, since Tracy seemed more at ease with her. "This is important. When you went out, did one of you, especially Jennifer, ever get a traffic ticket?"

"Yes, my God, we were scared," Tracy said. "We were leaving the Midnight Sun when a cop pulled us over. We were in Cody's car. The boys were at a men's bar, and we were on our way back to pick them up. Jennifer wasn't drunk, but we'd been drinking and we're underage. Even if all he did was give us a traffic ticket, we'd have to explain to our parents what we were doing in Dallas. We were so scared that Jennifer showed him her real driver's license. To our relief, he let her go with a warning. We laughed about it all the way home. In fact, I have the ticket. I kept it as a keepsake."

"You have the ticket?" Lauren leaned over the table.

"Yes, at home."

"Can we follow you there and get it?"

"Sure," Tracy said, looking puzzled.

"Could you recognize the police officer if you saw him again?" Lauren asked, handing her the composite drawing prepared by the Mexican road crew.

"No, I really never saw his face. I might recognize his voice."

"What about the car?"

"It had red and blue flashing lights. It looked like any police car."

"What was Jennifer wearing?" Lauren asked.

Tracy smiled but fought back tears. "A black sleeveless sheer blouse over red leggings."

"What about footwear, and did she wear fingernail polish?"

"Her nails were like mine, short because of basketball, but she liked to keep hers painted. That night she wore bright red to match the leggings. Her shoes were black heels."

Lauren drove quietly most of the way home. Maris thought about the kids and stared at the warning ticket that Tracy had given them. A slight odor of perfume clung to the white paper. It looked so harmless. Yet it was a ticket to death.

155

Lauren cleared her throat. "I've been thinking. We have to set a trap next Saturday night. We know it's a police officer or someone impersonating a police officer who stops women as they leave the Midnight Sun. If he stops me, the task force will bust him. We have enough evidence for a search warrant once we ID him."

"I don't think it'll work. I think he's watched me close enough to know who you are. What we may have to do is issue a warning statement."

"I've been thinking about that." She shifted in the driver's seat and stretched her neck. "Let's take it easy tonight and rest. I'll even cook."

"You mean I'm finally going to find out if you're any good in the kitchen. This is a major event."

"I'm afraid that once you find out, I'll have to cook all the time. But I'm desperate. I'm tired of fish sticks, green beans and macaroni and cheese. I think that and steak is all you know how to fix."

"Bullshit, I have a wonderful recipe for beanie weenies. And chili — I make a killer chili." The house was in sight when Maris added, "I'm really hurt. I thought you liked fish sticks, green beans and macaroni and cheese."

Turning into the driveway, Lauren laughed. "Honey, I love you, but I hate fish sticks."

Chapter Fourteen

Maris pulled on the red Texas Gay Rodeo Association T-shirt. After wasting three hours in federal court in Sherman waiting to testify, she needed a strenuous workout. They never had called her to the stand and she had to return Tuesday morning. It had taken some sweet talk, but she'd finally convinced the prosecutor to let her wait until one o'clock to appear. It gave her enough time to finish the D1S80 DNA typing on the fingernail and the other samples. The results verified those obtained from the DQ-alphas — Hatcher was eliminated but all of the other samples were from the same man. She had faxed a report to the task force office before leaving for court.

After baby-sitting Earnhardt outside for a few minutes, she rode her stationary bicycle for ten miles before attacking her free weights. Damn it, she thought struggling with her last bench press, she didn't want to go back to Sherman. Unfortunately, federal judges tended to lose their sense of humor when witnesses failed to show up. Gradually she sweated off her anger, and by the time she finished the treadmill, she had forgotten court and was thinking about Lauren and supper. After winding down with fifteen minutes of stretching exercises, she called it quits. She discovered Lauren sprawled on the couch reading the *Dallas Morning News* with Earnhardt curled up on the other end.

"Hello, any breaks today?" She frowned at Earnhardt. "And who said you could get on the couch?" Flopping on Lauren, she crumpled the newspaper beneath her and began kissing Lauren's neck. Earnhardt grunted and slowly, stretching between steps, climbed down from the sofa.

Lauren giggled, pushing against Maris's chest. "I thought you wanted to hear what we found out today."

"I do. Tell me."

"Not until you get off of me."

"Okay, I need a drink of water anyway." Maris grumbled, scrambling to her feet.

"Wait. I didn't mean now. Come back and kiss my neck some more."

"Woman, make up your mind." Maris laughed as she scooped some ice into a glass. Lauren sat up on the sofa and tried to straighten her paper. "Daniel Westmoreland said that the ticket Tracy Roper gave us is definitely not Dallas police department issue. And they're very curious about how we found out the women were lesbians. I explained about the names in Cynthia Allen's address book. I'm afraid Sally and I are using you for cover."

"Gee, thanks, darling, but I don't think it's going to help you much since we have the same address and phone number. Especially the way you blush every time I come into the task force office."

"I do not."

"Sure you do. I'll drop by after court tomorrow and show you."

"Seriously, Sally's sweating it. After all, she has to go back to work in Tyler when this is over."

"I know. You cooking again tonight?" Maris asked, perusing the refrigerator.

"See, I knew it. Cook once for a butch and they expect it every night."

"That's not all I expect every night."

"I have something to show you." Lauren laid two pieces of paper on the kitchen bar. "I brought home a copy of Cynthia Allen's speeding ticket and the warning ticket issued to Jennifer Belton. Look at the handwriting." She turned on the overhead light.

"We need Shannon for this. Amateur opinion only, but I'd say they were written by different people."

"That's what I think."

"The name of the officer is different on each ticket. Have you checked them out?"

"Yes, the officer on Cynthia Allen's speeding ticket is no longer with Austin P.D. We're trying to track him down. The name on the warning ticket is fictional, as far as we can tell. The one person by that name in Dallas is black and eighty-two years old." Lauren rolled her eyes. "Albert Wheeler is going back to Austin tomorrow. He'll take the tickets to Austin DPS lab for questioned documents to compare the handwriting. We can't afford to use Shannon." Lauren raised an eyebrow. "I doubt if she'll cut us the same deal she does you." She bumped her hip against Maris.

"I have a feeling you'll put panties on a bull calf before I get Shannon's help again."

"She knows what happened wasn't your fault."

"I hope so. I've been worried about her." She rubbed the condensation that had dripped from her glass onto the bar. "What about Debbie Keisler? We need to know if she had any police contact before she was killed."

"Al's looking into it. Our computer guy told Ralph it took longer than he expected, but he managed to prioritize the list of buyers from the U. S. Militia catalogue using your offender profile and eliminated, for now, all known females and non-white males as well as white males over fifty and under thirty. We're running criminal background checks on the remaining names to see if anyone leaps out at us and we're also comparing the list of Austin buyers from 'seventy-nine and 'eighty with the names of north Texas buyers for the last two years."

"Maybe he'll get a break."

"We're due one. I finally finished the paperwork

on the victim profiles and the crime scenes, typed up the VICAP Crime Analysis report and sent them off today."

"They should be able to tell us if there are any similar cases in another state."

"Hopefully." Lauren picked up the speeding tickets and sat down on a stool. Taking a piece of paper from her pocket, she handed it to Maris. "I hope Jeff Bell gets the court order for the Mail Shoppe records today."

"Jesus, what's taking him so long? I thought he'd already have them."

"He's had a lot to do checking all of the victim backgrounds. Have you heard what the media is calling the case?"

"No, but I can guess." Maris leaned tiredly on the bar.

"The 'Red Nails, Black Heels Murders.'"

Maris winced. It made the women sound so cheap. She took a long drink of ice water.

"We're releasing the DNA results tomorrow clearing Hatcher."

"I'm going to call Barbara and tell her. I don't want her reading it first in the newspapers." Maris drummed her fingers on the bar. "I'm afraid the publicity is going to trigger him into acting sooner."

"But none of the victims were taken before the twentieth of the month."

"He set fire to my truck after the *Austin Statesman* ran their first story. He killed Shannon's horse after we found the bodies. I've read of other serial killers changing their pattern, upping the frequency of attacks as the pressure increases. Remember Ted Bundy's attack on the dormitory in Florida? We need to put out a warning for any women who have received warning tickets near the gay bars."

"We've talked about it. Wayne thinks it's too soon. We don't want to blow our chance to trap him Saturday. Also, he wants to see what Al and Jeff turn up."

"I think we're obligated to do it soon. Can't we at least warn the bar owners?"

"I'll talk to Wayne again tomorrow. Maybe we'll get him before we have to make that decision. Want to help me go through the photos and videos from the funerals?"

"Sure, why not? I'm going to call Barbara Shelton first."

"Okay, I'm going to change. Let's call in pizza."

Maris nodded. She cracked open her black billfold and read Barbara's number off of a scrap of paper. An answering machine picked up on the second ring and Maris left a message for her to call.

She helped Lauren spread the photographs across the coffee table and dropped to the floor beside her. They worked in silence for several minutes studying the pictures, looking for a man who may have attended all of the funerals. Tired of looking at the photographs, Lauren called in a pizza delivery order and started the videotape. Maris watched attentively, especially the services she didn't attend. Nothing struck her as interesting until the camera panned the parking lot at Katherine Galimore's funeral. She grabbed the remote control and backed up the tape.

"Look at this Chevrolet Blazer, the red and white

one. I swear I saw one just like it at Jennifer's funeral." Maris paused the tape and searched through the photographs. "There — it is the same one. Check the plate."

Lauren unzipped the case on her lap-top computer and handed a telephone cord to Maris. "Hook this to your lab phone line." Within minutes she was logged into the FBI's secured computer system and running the license plate number. "It belongs to Bill Rogers," she said. Squinting at the screen, she clicked diligently on the keyboard. "According to his driver's license, he's six-one with brown hair and eyes. About one hundred and eighty pounds, forty-seven years old."

"That only describes half of the males in these photographs. Maybe he was there in an official capacity."

"Look for a man with a camera. Great idea." Lauren excitedly shuffled the photographs. She handed one to Maris. "He's in the background near the top corner." Maris saw a man in a green knit golf shirt with blue jeans and a camera around his neck. "That's Katherine Galimore's funeral. This looks like his green shirt sleeve on the edge of the picture. Phyllis Pierson's funeral was the same day."

"Here he is at Jennifer's funeral in the back corner again. We barely caught him in this frame." The time limit on the VCR pause ran out and Star Trek's *Voyager* roared across the television screen at warp speed. Maris jumped for the remote control and lowered the volume.

Lauren leaned against the sofa. "It's the same man in at least two of them, and he fits Bill Rogers' description."

The telephone rang and Maris beat Lauren to it, flashing a triumphant grin. She expected Barbara Shelton and was surprised by Shannon Stockwell's sultry voice. "I'm sorry about Buster," Maris said, relieved to hear from her. "I should've anticipated he would do something like that, but I didn't and I'm really sorry."

"It wasn't your fault. You can't blame yourself for something a monster like that does." Shannon sighed. "You were a good friend when I needed you."

"Some help I was."

"Robin and I left for Fort Lauderdale last Wednesday and flew back Sunday. We spent a lot of time walking on the beach and talking. Maybe we've solved some problems . . . only time will tell."

"I hope it works out the way you want it to. Where are you? You're not staying at home, are you?"

"Some good has already come out of this. The sheriff once bought several horses from my brother and they've become close friends. When the sheriff told him what happened, he tried to find me and left several messages in my voice mail and a note on the front door. I called him when we got back and my sister-in-law insisted that we stay with them. You don't know how nice it feels to have some family again."

"Hang in there, girl. The rest of them will come around."

"I hope so. Some photographer keeps calling the office and leaving messages. He says he's doing the photography for a true crime book on this case and wants a picture of Buster and the barn. I told him to go to hell."

Maris signaled to Lauren who was studying the videotape again. "What was the photographer's name?"

"Something Rogers."

"Bill Rogers?"

"I believe that's right, why?"

"Stay away from him, Shannon. He was the DPS photographer during the nineteen eighty murder investigations. Lauren and Wayne have been trying to find him. Did he leave a phone number?"

"Sure, hold on." Maris heard her set the telephone down. Within a few seconds, she returned and read off the number, which Maris repeated for Lauren to write down. "Are you considering him a suspect?"

"Sounds far out, but he's been accused of inappropriate behavior toward two women he photographed. I read about a paramedic that killed women and left their bodies in his assigned area so he could be the one to pick them up in the ambulance and carry them to the morgue. I guess it added to the thrill. Don't take any chances, Shannon. Call the task force if he comes to see you or calls again." They said good-bye and Maris set down the phone.

Earnhardt announced the presence of the pizza man before he could ring the doorbell. As Maris paid him, she realized she was hungrier than she thought. She wolfed down three pieces of the pepperoni, sausage and onion pizza and watched Lauren type on the lap-top with one hand while she nibbled on a thin slice of the pizza.

"The phone number is for the Motel 6 in Arlington. I think it's the one near Six Flags Over Texas." She swallowed a bite. "This is the last time I let you choose the toppings. I'll be up half the night with either indigestion or bad dreams. Hand me the phone. Since I'll be awake anyway, I might just go visit Mr. Rogers." Asking for the manager, she identified herself as FBI. Moments later, she put down the receiver. "He checked out at four-thirty this afternoon. I'm putting out an 'attempt to locate' on him with instructions to inform the task force of his position, if found."

Maris finished her fourth piece. "Too bad we missed him. I guess now we'll have to find something else to do — as long as you can't sleep anyway."

Chapter Fifteen

It was high noon Tuesday when the federal judge excused Maris from further testimony and she felt lucky to escape that early. Since the task force was having difficulty keeping up with the paperwork and manning the 800 number, despite Viola's ten-hour days, Maris decided to drop in and offer assistance.

Entering the cluttered office, she acknowledged Viola's greeting, but her attention riveted to Lauren and Sally Trent. Leaning against a filing cabinet, they intently studied a folder. They seemed to be standing a little closer than necessary, but when

Lauren spied Maris, her eyes brightened and she came to greet her. As she approached, she pushed open her emerald floral-patterned cardigan and stuck a hand into the pocket of her beige trousers. A slight blush crept up her neck, turning her cheeks crimson in sharp contrast to her white blouse. Eat your heart out, Sally Trent, Maris thought, grinning at Lauren.

"Damn you, Maris Middleton," Lauren whispered, "what are you using, subliminal suggestions or sorcery?"

"I save sorcery for the laboratory." She squeezed Lauren's hand once and released it.

"I called Barbara Shelton as you asked. I told her you wanted to tell her the results of the DNA yourself, but you were tied up in court."

"Thanks. How did she take it?"

"She asked several questions about your tests that I couldn't answer, but she seemed resigned to the outcome. She said it was hard to give up on Hatcher after all these years. She may call you later."

Sally waved a piece of paper at her. "Things are hopping today, Maris. Al Wheeler called from Austin. One of the orders for Eagle boots on the nineteen eighty list was placed by the same Austin policeman who wrote the traffic ticket to Cynthia Allen. He's no longer with Austin P.D. but Al's looking for him."

"And we found Robert Keisler," Lauren said. "Ralph Lambert's checking him out. At the time of his wife's death, he was a mechanic at a Ford dealership in Austin. After the murder, he started drag racing locally until he landed a job as a crew member for an NHRA team. After the owner dissolved the team in August, Keisler moved to Ennis and opened an engine shop."

"Ennis is where the big drag strip is located," Maris said.

Sally nodded. "His garage is not far from the track. He still races. Ralph contacted the owner of the team he used to work for. He told Ralph that Keisler never recovered from the loss of his wife. He talked about her frequently but seemed more upset about losing her to those 'brain-washing, evil lesbians,' quoting Keisler's words. He builds engines for a group of police officers who race dragsters with an anti-drug, anti-gang message."

"If Keisler is the murderer, why did he go fifteen years before he started killing again? It doesn't make sense."

"We don't know that he did," Sally said. "He's traveled all over the country while racing and could have victims scattered anywhere."

Lauren dropped into a desk chair. "Suppose he killed Debbie in a rage for leaving him for a woman and he killed Cynthia Allen to throw the blame onto a serial killer. He may not have felt the need to kill again until the race team dissolved, triggering his rage."

"Lauren, I think you're reaching. How did he know Cynthia Allen was a lesbian?" Maris asked.

"We wondered that also." Lauren smiled at Sally. "When I had Barbara Shelton on the phone this morning, I asked her what kind of car Cynthia drove. She had a Ford Mustang that was purchased at the dealership where Keisler worked. And he fits the profile you have for the killer and your theory about the traffic tickets. He owns a Chevrolet Suburban and a wrecker, but he works on police cars for the city of Ennis and Ellis County S.O. and could have access to a police vehicle on weekends. Ralph says there's a white Ford Crown Victoria in the shop now."

"Anyone seen him wearing Eagle boots?"

"Not yet." Lauren shrugged. "He favors the composite drawing made by the road crew. Ralph and Daniel have him under surveillance. It's all circumstantial, but the little things add up."

"What about Bill Rogers? Any luck locating him?"

Sally rolled and unrolled the paper in her hand. "He's moved everything out of his apartment in Houston. We found out that he owes twelve thousand dollars in child support to his second wife. That's probably why he's in hiding. We'll find him."

Maris took off her jacket and tossed it on the back of a chair. "I came to help with the chores around here. What can I do?"

"Check our e-mail," Lauren said. "Sally and I haven't had time. Print out everything. Anything hot, let us know."

Maris took a soft drink out of the refrigerator and sat down at the computer. There was more activity on the task force's Web page and more e-mail messages than she expected. She printed the messages and read them carefully. Several were from reporters seeking inside information. Two messages, obviously from devoted fans of the *X-Files*, informed her that creatures from outer space were responsible and blamed an FBI cover-up. There was one confession with a follow-up request that the police wait until his parents leave for work to arrest him. She shook her head, glad to have reached the next-to-last e-mail message. It brought her to the edge of her chair.

"Lauren, listen to this: 'Let me give you a hand for your nice Web page. I'd be a real heel if I didn't compliment you on your bright red logo. Nice. But all your horsing around won't stop me. Your fucking lesbian task force will never catch me.' " Lauren gripped the back of her chair and leaned over her shoulder. Maris scowled. "Does he mean task force investigating the death of lesbians, or does he mean lesbians on the task force?"

"It has to be him," Lauren said. "Can we trace the e-mail?"

"If it can be done at all, it'll be difficult. All a person has to do is open an anonymous e-mail account. This is done easily on the Internet, and you don't even have to use your real name or provide an address. You pay with a money order that you can sign with any name you want. It doesn't have to be your real one. Then any messages from the anonymous e-mail account are sent through a remailer — an Internet site that forwards the message to its destination and conceals the sender's e-mail address. To be really careful, a person could use several layers of anonymous e-mail accounts and remailers. There's even an encryption program to make it more secure called PGP — Pretty Good Privacy. I looked into this one time for a narcotics agent who was curious about how the crooks post instructions on the Internet for building bombs and cooking dope in a way that law enforcement can't trace the source. It seems to be almost untraceable, but you need to see if one of your FBI computer experts can do it."

Sally answered one of the ringing telephones. "It's Wayne for you, Maris."

"I had a deputy bring Brian Blake down from the mental hospital in Wichita Falls this morning," Wayne said in his slow drawl. "The crazy SOB. That whack to the head you gave him with the ax handle damn sure didn't knock any sense into him. I'm afraid the law hasn't heard the last from Brian Blake."

"Someday I'm going to regret not killing the little bastard while I had the chance."

"I talked to his family when they came up to the jail. His mother and sister admitted to me that they had a male boarder rooming with them for a couple of weeks in August until he found a place of his own. I'm not happy we missed this little tidbit of information during the Beauchamp investigation."

"Who was the boarder?"

"A man by the name of Dennis Wright. He was supposedly in the pen with Jessie Blake, one of Brian's uncles, but I can't find a record for a Dennis Wright with TDC that seems to fit what we know about him. Maybe it's an alias. I showed them a copy of the composite drawing Daniel got from the road crew and they say it sort of looks like him."

"What about Jennifer Belton? Did the women know her or see her with him?"

"No, but they were in Lubbock, working a temporary job for another relative during August. I checked out their story, and it's good. I tried to interview the little girl again, but it was too upsetting for her and her counselors broke it off before we finished. Tell Lauren I'm faxing in a report of my interviews and ask her to start a computer search for Dennis Wright, probably an alias. Also for Jessie Blake — no one knows where he is."

"If that's Wayne, I need to talk to him." Lauren

leaned on the edge of the desk with a sheet of fax paper in her hand.

"Wayne," she said when Maris handed her the telephone, "I've got new information on David Keisler. He was arrested for assault in San Jose eighteen months ago. I talked to the arresting officer and he faxed me a copy of the arrest report. Keisler had an altercation in a restaurant with two lesbian couples. A fight ensued outside the restaurant and he beat up one woman and spent the night in jail. He was released when the charges were dropped the next day." Excitement was creeping into Lauren's voice as she gestured with the sheet of paper. "I have a fax from the FBI crime analysis unit. They report a murder similar to ours in Los Angeles last July." Covering the telephone, she turned to Maris, "Do you have an NHRA schedule at home? We need to know if they raced in California in July."

"I can tell you now. I think I have one in my wallet on the back of a Winston Cup schedule. If I don't, we can access NHRA on the Internet." Maris fumbled with her wallet and pulled out a credit card-sized schedule. "The Autolite Nationals were in Sonoma, California, the last week of July."

"Sonoma, California, in July," Lauren repeated to Wayne.

Slamming down the receiver, she said, "I'll call Ralph and Daniel. Wayne wants them to pick up Keisler immediately for questioning and prepare a photographic lineup for us to show the road crew. If we get an ID, we're going to ask for a search warrant for Keisler's shop and home."

* * * * *

The hum of computers made Maris restless as she paced around the small task force office. Viola, grateful that Maris stayed to answer the phone, worked frantically to catch up on reports. The phones were surprisingly quiet for a couple of hours and Maris was glad when a ringing telephone broke the monotony. Al Wheeler asked for Wayne or Lauren. "They went to Ellis county to bring Keisler in for questioning."

"Debbie Keisler's husband? You've got to be kidding!"

"No, if some of the guys from the road crew pick him out of a photo lineup, they plan to get a search warrant."

"I can't believe it's him. The lead I've got — thanks to your tip on the boot manufacturer — is too good to ignore." He cleared his throat and Maris heard his voice vibrate with suppressed tension. "The officer, Ray Sanchez, who wrote Cynthia Allen's traffic ticket, was on the list from the catalogue company. He ordered several pairs of the Eagle boots for a junior police cadet program sponsored by Austin P.D. It was an experimental program for troubled boys. One of the cadets, Donnie Wade Baker, was riding with Ray Sanchez when he wrote Cynthia Allen's speeding ticket."

"So this Baker kid could have seen her address on the ticket?"

"Yes, and there was a women's gay bar only a couple of blocks from where Sanchez stopped Cynthia. Two weeks before Debbie Keisler died, Sanchez and Baker answered a call at her house and took a complaint about a burglary of her vehicle. Sanchez remembers that she had some woman hanging all over her. Their relationship was obvious. He and the kid laughed about it after they left. Call them and tell them to forget Keisler. Baker's our boy. In nineteen eighty, he beat his grandmother to death with a baseball bat. He was sentenced to twenty-five years, but with good time, he was released June first."

"Damn, that's just in time for our murders to start."

"I don't know about the boots, though. He's not likely to still have his cadet boots."

"No, but this guy's a cop freak. And he's trying to impersonate an officer when he writes the warning tickets, and those boots are popular with the police. He's already familiar with the brand and he'd likely buy another pair."

"My dad signed out the burglary report two and a half years ago. That's probably how he knew Hatcher was innocent. I'm faxing the report on Donnie Wade's arrest and a photograph. He resembles the composite, but the picture is from nineteen eighty. I'm trying to get his prison records. If we can get an address on this bastard, we're in business."

"I'll start searching for a telephone number and address. Wayne has information that a man recently released from prison named Dennis Wright was staying with the Blake family when their foster child reported witnessing a rape."

"Might be an alias for Donnie Wade, using his first two initials. Call Wayne for me."

"What about Donnie Wade's relatives? Maybe they know where to find him."

"The father was a truck driver killed in an accident in 'seventy-eight. Don't know why, but the father and grandmother had legal custody of Donnie and his sister. Haven't found the sister or mother yet."

When Al hung up, Maris paged Lauren. While she waited for her to call back, she told Viola about Al's call and asked her to start searching for information on Donnie Wade Baker and/or Dennis Wright. Almost an hour passed before Lauren returned her call. "Hello, lover," she said, her voice quivering from adrenaline. "What do you need?"

"Lauren, Al Wheeler called. The Austin police officer on the catalogue list ordered several pairs of Eagle boots for a police cadet program. One of the cadets was with him when he gave the ticket to Cynthia Allen and took a burglary report from Debbie Keisler. This cadet went to the pen in 'eighty for killing his grandmother and was released in June."

Lauren interrupted. "Maris, it sounds intriguing, but two of the men on the road crew picked Keisler's photo out of the picture lineup. We're writing up the search warrant now. Try to find Jeff Bell and ask him to come to the S.O. as soon as possible. We'll wait for him to run the warrant. Also, call Al and tell him to return to Dallas tomorrow. We want to concentrate all resources on Keisler."

"Donnie Wade's background ties in with our profile of the murderer perfectly."

"But the road crew puts Keisler in the vicinity of the bodies shortly before Theresa Eastin was dumped in another location."

"Daniel said none of the men spoke fluent English. There could be a misunderstanding or they may simply be trying to please the police. You know eyewitness identifications are notoriously inaccurate."

"That's not all we have. I'll follow through on Al's information, if for no other reason than to eliminate Baker as a suspect so Keisler can't use him as a defense strategy. I have to go now. We'll talk later."

You bet, Maris thought, feeling summarily dismissed. She paged Jeff Bell. While she was waiting for him to phone in, she called Al Wheeler and told him to return to Dallas.

"Damn, I can't believe it's Keisler. It doesn't make sense."

"No, it doesn't, but I hope they're right." She refrained from adding, "Although I know they're not."

"Before I leave Austin, I'm going by Baker's old house where he lived with his grandmother and talk to some of the neighbors. I'll ask if they know where to find the sister or mother."

"Good luck, Al," she said, hanging up the telephone. Jeff Bell walked into the task force office, startling Maris. "Did you page me?" he asked. "I was so close I decided I could be here by the time I called."

"They're getting ready to run a search warrant on David Keisler's home and want you to meet them at Ennis P.D." He dropped into a chair with his mouth open. She explained the evidence against Keisler and told him about Al Wheeler's new suspect. As he prepared to leave, Maris asked, "Did you talk to the people at the Mail Shoppe in Tyler?"

"No, my son got into a little trouble at school and I had to meet with the teacher and principal. I did get the court order for their records. I was dropping by here to check for messages and then heading to Tyler."

Maris glanced at clock. It was almost four o'clock. "What time do they close?"

"Six."

If she left now, she could just make it. "Give me the court order and address for the Mail Shoppe."

"I don't know —"

"We have to tie up all loose ends. Maybe Keisler mailed the package to me. Or maybe Donnie Wade Baker did. We have to know."

He reached into the breast pocket on his suit and handed her an envelope. "Everything is in there, including a photocopy of the numbers on your package. Good luck. Let me know what you find out."

Maris thumbed through the papers in the envelope. "Should you be doing this?" Viola asked after Jeff left. She watched Maris with concern as she brushed a loose strand of gray hair from her forehead.

"Probably not." Maris smiled and winked. "But it's a nice day for a drive."

Chapter Sixteen

Maris flew past the strip mall with an H.E.B. grocery and several small stores including the Mail Shoppe. Checking the side mirror, she slammed on the brakes, skidded into a sharp U-turn and cut the Ford truck hard, sliding into the parking lot. Ten minutes before closing time, she greeted the attractive blond behind the counter and asked for the manager.

"Present and accounted for." She smiled. "I'm Becky Rider, the owner-manager, janitor and general flunky. What can I do for you?" Maris noticed the wedding ring on her finger and a picture of two boys and a handsome man holding up a string of catfish. Hopelessly hetero, she decided, but definitely attractive. She guessed her age to be about forty.

Flashing what she hoped was her most beguiling grin, Maris said, "I'm with the task force working on the Pierce county murders. I received a package that we traced back to your store using the UPS delivery code." Maris handed her the court order and the copy of the codes on the package.

"I've been expecting someone. I'm sorry I couldn't release this information without a court order. My lawyers . . ." She rolled her eyes and waved Maris into the back room. She opened a file drawer. "This is the paperwork for all of the packages mailed UPS on Christmas Eve. We were really busy that day." She shuffled the pages. "Here it is. The papers for that tracking number. This is filled out by the customer." She glanced at the form and jerked her head up. Maris thought she saw a hint of fear in her eyes. Becky recovered quickly and said, "This guy was one of our regulars."

"Tell me about him." Maris took the document from her using a pair of tweezers that she removed from her shirt pocket. It was a long shot, but there might be fingerprints left on the form from their boy. She saw the customer's name listed as Dan Wilson. At least he was consistent with his initials although she wondered why he dropped his last name and initial. *Middleton Forensic Services* and the laboratory address were listed as the intended recipient of the package.

"Don't worry about fingerprints." Becky shook her head. "He always wears driving gloves — even when it's warm outside. And he uses the mailbox he rents from us as his address, so that won't help you much. I've never called the home number he listed there, but he recently gave me a different number —" She looked around her desk for a slip of paper. Finding it, she handed it to Maris. "He said he was working at this number temporarily and asked me to call him when an order he was waiting for arrived. I did but kept the number in case I needed to call him again." She leaned against the filing cabinet. "We actually made a mistake on the transaction you're interested in. He told us specifically not to mail it UPS like we normally do his stuff. He wanted it sent U. S. Mail. I had several high-school girls working here through the holidays. One of them messed up and mailed it UPS despite his request. He received his bill last week and he was furious when he saw our mistake. He frightened me . . . I thought he might hit me. I was reaching for the phone to call nine-one-one when another customer walked in. He calmed down and apologized. I'm glad the girls weren't here. He'd have scared them to death. He called later and canceled his mailbox. He hasn't mailed any more packages and nothing has arrived for him." She shrugged. "I don't miss him as a customer after that last incident."

"What did he usually mail?"

"Computer equipment. Boards, computer parts. He told me he was a computer consultant and repaired computers, customized systems for businesses and helped them set up networks. You know, if we had mailed this package using stamps as he wanted it, you wouldn't have been able to trace it."

"I guess we were lucky." Maris showed her the composite drawing. "Does he look like this?"

"Kind of, but his face is fuller and the neck thicker. The nose is close, but not quite right."

Maris drove slower on the return trip. She was almost home when the car phone rang. "Hello, lover," Lauren said.

"I'm glad you called. I followed up on the Mail Shoppe. I think I have a good phone number for the guy who mailed the package. The name he used was —"

"That's intriguing, but we found the hands — from the old murders, we think, not the most recent — in a box in Keisler's closet. They're dry, mummified and relatively well-preserved."

Maris gripped the steering wheel. "Were there any goddamn prints on the box?"

"We don't know yet, but we're having it checked."

Trying not to lose her temper, Maris took a deep breath. "Have you found his torture room?"

"He has a large storeroom off of his shop where we think he may have taken the women. We'd like you to luminol it, the shop and his house. See if you can find any blood."

"Hell, yes, I'd like to luminol his place." She couldn't fucking believe that they'd found the hands in Keisler's closet. "I have to run by the lab and get some supplies. That'll take about twenty minutes."

She glanced at her watch. "Have someone meet me at Ennis P.D. at about nine-thirty." It was going to be another long night.

"Lauren, doesn't it disturb you that there were no fingerprints on the box with the hands?" Cradling a cup of coffee, Maris leaned against the dresser in their bedroom. She was tired and about half pissed. They hadn't finished at the Keisler premises until after two. It was four o'clock before they collapsed in bed, and then it felt like there was an invisible barrier between them. She suspected that Lauren had felt it too, and they tried to erase it with a round of passionate love-making when they finally woke up at ten o'clock. "Why weren't the hands from the Pierce county bodies there also? What about the torture room that no one could find? We went over every inch of Keisler's house, shop and storeroom with luminol and found no traces of blood."

"Get off it, Maris. I know there are holes in the evidence."

"I even checked all of Keisler's clothes and the washer for blood and found nothing, except for traces of blood on his shop clothes. Not unusual for a mechanic, I'd say." She sat on the side of the bed next to Lauren's suitcase. It seemed like Lauren was always leaving and she was always the disgruntled lover watching her go. It was not a promising pattern.

"I know. That's why Wayne called Huntsville to get Donnie Wade Baker's latest prison photo. When they faxed us a copy, we sent Jeff and Ralph back to the Blake house in Pierce county to see if David Wright could have been Baker."

Although it was almost two o'clock on Wednesday afternoon, Maris sipped her first cup of coffee and tried to hold her temper. Was it her imagination, or did the fragrance of sex still permeate the room? Despite a shower, she smelled Lauren's scent lingering on her fingertips. Any minute, the shuttle would arrive to take Lauren to the airport. And they were still arguing. What was this case doing to them?

"I'm glad you're going to California. It makes sense to investigate the murder there in July and find out if Keisler was in the area at that time. But I want you to do me a favor — make sure the victim has no connection to Austin or Donnie Wade Baker."

"Okay, lover," Lauren said tiredly. "I'll look into it. This investigation isn't closed, but —" The doorbell rang and she snapped her suitcase closed. "Why are you pushing this so hard? Won't the DNA analysis clear Keisler, if we're wrong?" Before Maris could say anything, she breezed by her with a peck on the check and a wave as she hurried to catch the airport shuttle.

Still sitting on the bed, Maris finished her coffee. Yes, she thought, DNA will clear Keisler — in about two fucking days. That was a lot of time. Time that could be spent hunting down Donnie Wade Baker. After rinsing her coffee cup and leaving it in the kitchen sink, she unlocked the laboratory and retrieved Keisler's blood from the refrigerator. Would history someday look back at the advent of forensic DNA as the demise of good, old-fashioned detective footwork? she wondered.

Chapter Seventeen

Groggy, Maris fumbled for the telephone. "Jesus, Shannon," she said, after the caller identified herself, "what the fuck time is it?"

"Five o'clock. You know I like to get an early start."

"I do too, but not this damned early. What do you want?"

"My, aren't we surly this morning. Where's Lauren? I was calling to tell her I have an appointment at nine to meet Bill Rogers at his apartment."

"You're not going!"

"No, but I thought Lauren or someone on the task force might be interested in attending."

"I'll take care of it. Give me the address and phone number." After writing down the information, Maris grumpily showered and dressed. No one was at the task force office yet. She called Al Wheeler's pager and ate breakfast while she waited for an answer. Damn it, if she had to meet Rogers, it would mess up the DNA test schedule on Keisler's blood. She piddled in a half-hearted attempt to organize her laboratory paperwork. Her billing procedures, so carefully planned, had gone straight to hell. Mary Ann, a CPA, and a good one, would have deleted the whole program and started over. Lauren had offered to help and inexplicably Maris had turned her down. Maybe she should reconsider, if their relationship survived this investigation. At a quarter to eight, she called Al's pager again. When there was still no reply, she checked her Dallas Mapsco for the best route to Bill Rogers' apartment and started on her way.

The apartment complex, located on East Grand, was not in the best part of Dallas. Trying to miss as many busted beer bottles as possible, Maris parked near a broken-down fifteen-year-old Monte Carlo and searched for apartment one-fifteen. She recognized him from the photographs taken at the funerals when he opened the door. Bowed slightly at the waist with hunched, rounded shoulders, he ran a hand nervously through his receding hairline and said, "You're not Shannon Stockwell."

Maris stepped past the peeling paint on the door into the dim apartment. A shadeless lamp lit up a tiny living room with one chair and a card table with an old 286 computer. One cracked wall was covered with photographs — some black and white, some color — of the 1980 crime scenes. Another wall was filled with color photographs from the funerals, including close-ups of a tear-streaked Tracey Roper leaning on Cody's shoulder. Other pictures depicted the front of a condominium, an empty parking lot at the University of North Texas and the empty drainage ditch where Theresa Eastin's body was discovered. Maris felt sick. Various other shots caught Wayne and Ralph in front of Pierce County S.O., Lauren and Sally in front of the task force office and Lauren and Maris outside of Keisler's shop. "I'm Maris Middleton," she finally said. "What the hell is all of this?"

"I thought I recognized you." After shoving a stack of newspapers out of the chair, he gestured for her to sit down. He unfolded a metal chair propped against the wall and plopped into it, lighting a cigarette. "My work," he said, waving at the walls. "I'm collaborating with an investigative reporter to write a book on the Red Nails and Black Heels Murderer — who, I might add, has a penchant for lesbians." He leaned forward, knocking his ashes into an empty beer can. "Something, I understand, you know a little about."

"No, I know a lot about it." She didn't try to hide the contempt in her voice. "So this is how you plan to pay off your child support and stay out of jail. Sensationalize these deaths by romanticizing a ruthless rape-murderer and playing up the erotic lesbian relationships of the victims. Real Pulitzer Prize material. Good luck getting any of these women to talk to a slimebag like you."

Rogers jumped to his feet. "I don't have to listen to this shit. For your information, we're close to getting a six-figure advance. What the fuck do you want anyway?"

"You've already answered most of my questions." She casually stood and stretched. "Just for the record, though, where were you from . . ." She shrugged. "Let's say August through Christmas."

"It's really none of your fucking business, but I was in Bosnia from July until mid-November. Sold some pictures to *Newsweek*, so I'm not your killer. But you knew that."

"Yes, I know that. You're about one step up from him on the evolutionary scale." She pulled a Ziplock baggie out of her pocket with a sealed foil wrapper containing a sterile wipe, a lancet and a cotton swatch. "Since you're such a great journalist and so cooperative with the police, I don't suppose you'd mind donating a little blood." She tore open the package with the sterile wipe. "Stick out your finger." He made an obscene gesture and turned the fingertip upright in front of her. She rubbed it with the sterile wipe and punctured it none too gently with the lancet. He winced slightly when she squeezed his finger to collect a large drop of blood but didn't complain. Holding the cotton swab by the edge, she dropped it into a plastic petri dish that she removed from her other coat pocket. She said, "Leave Shannon the fuck alone." Without waiting for a reply, she left the apartment, slamming the door behind her with enough force to rattle the windows. Maybe with luck, she thought, the fucker would bleed to death from the prick on his finger.

* * * * *

She was still fuming as she opened the petri dish with Bill Rogers' blood under the hood for it to air dry. She was labeling the dish when Al Wheeler rang the laboratory doorbell. "I checked my messages at the task force office," he said. "Since I was close, I decided to stop and see what you needed." Sitting across from her at the desk where she usually received evidence, he scanned what he could see of the lab behind her. "This is nice."

Her anger returned as she told Al about her visit with Bill Rogers and his up-coming book.

He shook his head. "What a jerk. Sorry I didn't get the page. I dropped my pager yesterday and don't think it's working now." He yawned and shook his head again. "I'm tired. I drove into town last night and got up early this morning and drove to Denison to find Donnie Wade Baker's sister. Before I left Austin yesterday, I talked to the man who lives in the old Baker house now. He didn't know the Bakers and bought the house through an attorney representing the sister, Doris Gail Lofton. He told me an interesting story. Early this summer someone dug a large hole under his elm tree in the backyard. It destabilized the root system and the tree toppled over during a thunderstorm. He doesn't know why the hole was dug or who did it, but it happened in early June."

"Maybe Donnie Wade went back for his keepsakes."

"The hands and shoes. Yeah, that's what I think." He rubbed his chin. "I think he knew somehow that we were looking at Keisler and broke into his house to plant the hands."

"Yes, I agree. I don't know if he's bugged the task force office, followed us around or what, but he knows a lot about us. Did you have any luck finding the sister?"

"Oh boy, did I. She's a real sweetheart — cursed me up one side and down the other." Al rolled his dark brown eyes. "The house was full of marijuana roaches and empty beer cans. Claims she's afraid of her brother and swears she doesn't know where he lives. Says she's only talked to him once in the last two years, when he called to say he was getting out soon. Get this, he told her that he was opening some kind of computer consulting business. I checked with the prison and they confirmed that he's a real computer whiz. Learned it all in the pen. He'll probably be earning a living from computers some way. I called Jeff Bell to look into it since he's already looking to see if there's a computer connection with any of the victims."

"Did you ask Doris if Donnie Wade had any reason to hate lesbians?"

"She told me her father, a truck driver, came home early one night and caught their mother with another woman. He threw them both out of the house and later won a custody suit for the kids. They lived with him and their grandmother. He was a long hauler, gone most of the time, and the grandmother took care of them. When the father was killed in a wreck, she gained full custody of the kids. Doris says that the grandmother was very bitter toward her ex-daughter-in-law and hated queers. Talked constantly about how they should be struck down by the Lord and sent to burn in hell."

Maris shook her head. "Everything fits with this

guy. What else did she say about life with Grand-mother?"

"Just that her grandmother was too old and sick to be raising young children. Doris used to paint her and Donnie's nails red with their mother's polish, and they'd play dress up in the clothes she left behind. She says it made her feel close to her mother again. The grandmother caught them while Doris was in one of her mother's dresses and Donnie Wade was wearing her silk blouse with a pair of black heels. She ripped the blouse off of Donnie, beat them with a belt and drug them into the bathroom where she removed the fingernail polish. She stood Donnie Wade up in front of the mirror, jerked down his pants and told him, 'You have a penis. Boys do not wear dresses or women's shoes.' She spent the rest of the afternoon reading the Bible to him."

"We should write a book — *How to Fuck Up a Young Male*," Maris said, before excusing herself to get the information from the Mail Shoppe. "I haven't had a chance to take this to the task force office yet." She showed him the customer shipping infor-mation form for the package and the other number she'd been given. Picking up the telephone, she dialed the home number listed. "We have to find this guy."

The phone rang once and a computer voice said, "Welcome to AT&T Wireless Services. The cellular customer you have called is —"

Maris broke the connection. "Should have known from the number it was a mobile unit." Reading off the scrap of paper, Maris dialed the temporary work number their suspect had provided the Mail Shoppe and put the phone on speaker so Al could hear. Their eyes locked in surprise when a woman answered,

"Communications, Pierce County S.O., may I help you?"

Maris realized she didn't know what name Donnie Wade would be using. Acting on impulse, she said, "I didn't expect to reach the sheriff's office. I was looking for D.W."

"Is this about the main board he ordered for our server?"

Maris raised her eyebrows. The bastard has been working for the sheriff's office — unbelievable. "Yes, ma'am," she said, trying to keep an even voice. "There's a slight problem with his order. Is he there now?"

"No, he said he had a minor family emergency to attend to today and is unavailable. We don't expect him back until tomorrow. Maybe I can answer your questions."

"My assistant just handed me a note saying the problem has been taken care of. I'll see to it the board is shipped immediately. Thank you."

She realized Al had been holding his breath. "Jesus fucking Christ," he blurted. "He's working at the sheriff's office."

"Ralph told me when I was there last ..." She glanced at the calendar. "Back on the second, that someone was working on their computer systems." She slapped her forehead. "Oh goddamn, I've seen the bastard. He almost knocked me down with a ladder. He was busy running computer cable outside of Ralph's office. He probably heard Wayne talk about the first article that appeared in the *Austin Statesman*. Incredible. He had to have heard me tell them I was going to court in Fort Worth. He does resemble the composite drawing made by the road repair crew."

Al seemed visibly shaken. "That's how the fucker knows what the task force is doing. Ralph's been keeping the sheriff informed and the bastard is probably working where he can overhear dispatch." He waved the customer form from the Mail Shoppe. "Hopefully I can get his home address from AT&T Wireless. We've got to get hold of Wayne and Ralph. Warn the sheriff to pick him up if he returns to the S.O. to finish the job. And we better be damned sure he doesn't get any more information from us." Before Maris could hand him the phone, he jumped as his pager vibrated with an odd rattle. "I didn't think this was working at all." He looked at the display. "Only four numbers are showing, but I think it's for the task force office." He grabbed Maris's telephone. After a short delay, he identified himself and listened solemnly. Her stomach dropped when she saw the anguish in his grimace. He said, "We've already run out of time. We have another missing woman."

Chapter Eighteen

Grim faces filled the crowded task force office. Ralph, his face red with fury and embarrassment, paced between the front table and the filing cabinets. The sheriff had already been appraised of the situation and stood by with deputies to arrest Donnie Wade if he returned to the S.O. Maris sat slumped in a yellow plastic chair watching Sally Trent and Al Wheeler call the utility and telephone companies in north Texas trying to locate something in Donnie Wade's real name or any of the other names that they knew he had used. Al had already checked with

AT&T Wireless and the mobile number was a dead end. The tricky bastard had used yet another alias and the Mail Shoppe street address with his box number as a place of residence. Given enough time, Maris knew that they'd eventually stumble on to something — maybe a credit card or bank account in one of his many names and a paper trail to follow. Ultimately it would be the kidnapped woman who paid the price for any delay with pain and possibly her life.

Jeff paced the floor, and Daniel Westmoreland fidgeted in the chair next to Maris while they waited for Wayne to brief them on the missing woman. After taking a brief telephone call, he called for their attention.

"Her name is Lisa Anderson. She's a real estate agent and met a prospective client yesterday afternoon to look at some commercial property in north Dallas. Police found her abandoned car this morning after her roommate . . . partner reported her missing at seven o'clock this morning. Dallas P.D. immediately began a search. Daniel and I interviewed the roommate and confirmed that Lisa Anderson is a lesbian. Three weeks ago, she received a warning ticket for running a stop sign after leaving a Dallas gay bar."

Maris clenched her fist and slammed it against the palm of her other hand in frustration. Wayne passed around a photograph of a petite dark-haired woman, handsomely dressed, with brilliant blue eyes and a captivating smile. Maris felt physically ill when she saw the photograph. Her eyes met Sally's across the table. "He's had her over fifteen hours already," she whispered. "He can inflict a lot of pain in fifteen hours."

Sally nodded, staring at the picture. Wayne said, "We screwed up with David Keisler. Maris and Al believe that Donnie Wade Baker planted the hands we found." He explained how Al came up with Baker as a suspect using the information developed from the Eagle shoeprint. "He went to the pen in 'eighty for beating his grandmother to death with a baseball bat but got an early release in June."

Sally asked, "Why set Keisler up and then abduct another victim so soon? He knows this will clear him."

Wayne shrugged and Maris said, "He likes to play games. And the distraction kept us from issuing a warning to all of the women who may have received a bogus warning ticket from this bastard. If the Mail Shoppe had not failed to follow Donnie Wade's instructions, we wouldn't have had a tracking number on the package. There would be no way to find out where it was mailed from and we wouldn't even know he was working at the S.O. Too bad the fucker probably won't show up for work again. He probably hoped setting Keisler up would buy him time or maybe even make us overlook this evidence." She bolted upright. "Damn, call the S.O. and find out if the computer part he was waiting for has been delivered —"

Jeff stopped his pacing. "And if it has, get the name of the computer company and find out if they have a phone number, address or credit card number for the bastard. Maybe he orders from them frequently." He plopped into a desk chair, pulled out a pen and notepad and immediately started dialing the phone.

Wayne jerked up a phone ringing on another line.

Maris could tell it was Lauren by the way Wayne brought her up-to-date. "Okay, I'm putting you on the speaker phone," he said, pushing the button. "It's Lauren. She's on her way back, calling from the plane."

Maris heard the fatigue and worry in Lauren's voice. "It was worth the trip out here. The murder here was similar to ours except, by all indications, she was not a lesbian. No semen or blood was found on the body and the police had no suspects. I was beginning to think the similarities might be coincidence, but I promised Maris I'd look for connections to Austin or Donnie Wade Baker. I found them. His mother moved out here after she left Austin, but she died of breast cancer in early June. I talked to her lover — the same one she left Austin with. In July, she went on a trip with some friends. While she was gone, a man matching Donnie Wade's description showed up looking for his mother. Concerned neighbors told him she was dead. Later, someone broke into the house. Blood and feces were smeared on the walls, the furniture was trashed and pictures were destroyed. It was the same day the murder occurred. I think he planned to kill his mother and was furious when he found out she was already dead. The lover was gone so he couldn't take out his rage on her. I don't think this murder was planned. I think he came across the victim and she was an easy substitute for his mother — a way to vent his rage." It sounded like Lauren paused for a drink. "Maris, the lover is the spittin' image of you — only twenty-five years older. The resemblance is uncanny. I'll have a cab take me home from the airport so I can pick up my car. I'll check in with the task force again then.

Good luck." The dial tone sounded before Wayne cut the connection.

"I've got him," Jeff shouted, slamming down his phone as he leapt to his feet. "The part was delivered to the S.O. this morning. I called the computer company and they said he does a lot of business with them but usually bills back to the company he's working for at the time . . . like the S.O. in this order. But once he requested some information from them and gave them a fax number. I figured it'd be some business, but when I called Southwestern Bell and identified myself as a police officer, they gave me the address. It's a residence on Farm-to-Market Road seventeen about two miles southwest of Pierce. He gave both companies the name Dawson Wayne Brown."

Ralph frowned. "Could be the old Williams place? I heard someone had rented it a few months ago."

"Let's get to work on the search warrant. Lisa Anderson may not have much time," Wayne said.

The ordinary appearance of the yellow wood-frame farmhouse, the weathered barn and the tall pecan trees contrasted sharply with the horror they expected to find inside. An old green-and-rust colored Chevrolet pickup rested on a flat tire in front of the barn. No other vehicles were present. Out of sight of the house, two sheriff's cars blocked off each end of the road. When the signal was given, three cars stormed the house. Sally and Daniel in her black Chevrolet Caprice raced to the back of the house. Jeff, with a Pierce county deputy along for the ride, hurried to block the entrance to the barn. Following in her Ford pickup, Maris slid to a stop behind Ralph and Wayne and was two yards behind them when they crashed through the front door. Sally and Daniel covered the back door while Jeff and the deputy took the barn. Entry was smooth and safe, but Donnie Wade Baker was not home.

Maris was disappointed, but they couldn't back off and wait for him until they found Lisa Anderson. They scoured the house quickly, making sure it was empty. Ralph on the first pass found a pair of Eagle Sniper/Commando boots in a closet in the master bedroom. One glance at the left shoe revealed a deep slash on the third grid up from the logo. These were the right boots. A converted bedroom in the back corner of the house drew Maris's attention. As she surveyed the room, taking in the sophisticated computer equipment, blinking monitors, and stacks of software and computer catalogues, interspersed with piles of pornographic magazines and videotapes, she wondered if Donnie Wade had mastered the art of using stolen credit cards while in the pen. Flipping through the pornography, Maris saw bestiality, domination, rape and torture scenes. She dropped it in disgust when the growl of the hard drive on the main computer caught her attention. Curious, she hit the spacebar and the monitor came to life.

Break-in detected at 14:35, the text read. *Starting emergency sequence two 14:41.* She heard the hard drive whirl and watched the flashing green lights play on the front of the computer. She didn't like it. Then realization hit her — booby trap.

She shouted, "Get out of the house! Everyone out now!" She jabbed the power button on the front of the computer and it fell uselessly inside the computer box. "Goddamn," she said, knocking the monitor to one side as she lunged for the cables behind the computer.

She heard Wayne shouting for everyone to get out of the house as she ripped the cord to a crowded power strip out of the wall, hoping to kill the computer in time. But a bright flash and intense heat followed by blinding orange and yellow flames lashed out at her from a partially opened closet door. Wayne slammed into her, shoving her roughly to the floor. Rolling to her hands and knees, she fumbled through tangled cables and loose disks until she unplugged every electrical cable in the room. The inside of the closet was an inferno. Wayne shielded his face from the intense heat with crossed arms and kicked the door closed to retard the spread of the flames. Coughing, he stumbled down the hallway to the front porch with Maris close behind.

Ralph rushed past them with a fire extinguisher from his car and Sally followed with a green garden hose. "Goddamn, what was that?" Wayne asked, breathing heavily.

"My guess is a light bulb filled with gasoline. It's a little trick the old dope cooks liked to use to greet the police when their speed labs were raided. The computer was programmed to turn the light on in the closet. When the electrical current hit the gas . . . Boom!"

"We're both lucky that closet door was almost closed or we'd be crispy critters."

"Yeah," Maris said, fingering her singed hair. "The question is, what other little surprises did he have planned? I don't know if that was all or if I stopped the computer before anything else was activated."

Coughing, Ralph came out on to the porch and threw the empty fire extinguisher to the ground. "I don't know how, but we got the fire out. I could smell gasoline. Sally's running water on it to cool it down and keep it from reigniting."

Jeff and Daniel ran around the corner of the house, slowing when they reached the porch. "Everyone's fine," Wayne said. "He had the place booby-trapped. Luckily, Maris figured it out before too much damage was done."

She said, "It's interesting that he had the closet wired for destruction first. I think we need to get in there as soon as it's cool enough."

"She's right," Daniel agreed. "Before I heard the explosion, I was studying that side of the house. There's been a room added on the southwest corner. A room with no outside windows or doors. I was on my way in to check, but the only access to that room may be through the closet."

Wayne nodded, stepping off of the porch. "Jeff, check on Sally. She probably needs someone to relieve her. I'm calling the Dallas bomb squad. I want them here before we enter that room." Maris watched him slide into the open door of his car and pick up the radio.

Sally came out and dropped tiredly on the top step of the porch. "Lord, there's still a lot of heat coming out of there." Pulling the tail of her shirt out of her trousers, she wiped her face. "There's a steel door inside the closet with a metal bar padlocked across it."

Ralph talked quietly in his handheld radio. "I called the volunteer fire department, but they're already out on a big grass fire. They'll come help us pull the debris out of the way and cool it off when they're finished."

Maris couldn't stand the waiting. Lisa could be on the other side of the locked door injured and dying. A few minutes might make a difference.

Wayne stood up next to his car. "It'll be a couple of hours before the bomb boys can get here."

She stood up stiffly, slightly bruised from when Wayne shoved her to the floor. "I have a couple of shovels and two battery-powered spotlights in the back of the truck. Why don't I start shoveling some of the debris out the back window in the computer room? If there was an explosive device inside the closet, it probably would have gone off with the light bulb or from the action of the water."

"There's another hose in back," Daniel said, standing. "I'll make sure the debris doesn't ignite the grass back there. Everything around here is so fucking dry."

"Okay," Wayne agreed. "But don't try to get in the steel door until the bomb squad arrives."

"We're going to need a cutting torch," Sally said, rising from the top step. "I'll help Maris clear out the closet."

Wayne frowned. "I'll round up a cutting torch. You two be careful." He instructed Ralph and Daniel to search the grounds for any signs of recent digging or other traps.

Using the shovel, Maris broke the back window. Sally set up the spotlights and pointed them inside the smoky closet. She and Sally began to clear the debris, pulling out piles of smoldering computer paper and clothing while Jeff kept the water trained on the charred area. The ceiling was a concern, but Maris managed to knock down the damaged sheetrock. They had been lucky the flames hadn't spread to the attic. The whole house could have burned to the ground quickly.

Sweat was dripping off of Maris's nose, and her dark blue coveralls were wet and stained. Wet, black ashes coated her shoes. Soon they had a path cleared to the steel door. Jeff kept the water trained on the walls and floor until they were cool to the touch.

Wayne came into the room carrying a small cutting torch. "We're in luck. I found this in the barn. I tried it out; it works." He stepped inside the closet with Maris and carefully examined the door.

"Damn," Ralph said. Concern darkened his face. "The S.O. and DPS highway patrol are reporting grass fires all around us. The high wind is blowing from southwest to northeast driving the fires. The Old Settlers' Baptist Church, over a hundred and fifty years old, burned to the ground. The fires are widespread — someone's setting them. The rest home on the edge of town is in jeopardy. They're asking for any available hands to help fight the fires and evacuate the old folks. I sent Jeff Bell to see how close the fires are to us."

"That fucking bastard is probably setting them." Wayne barked, "Release the deputies helping us and tell Daniel to go with them. Help any way they can."

"It must really be bad," Ralph said, listening to his handheld radio. "They're asking for help from the Greenville and Tyler fire departments. All surrounding volunteer fire departments are already en route.

More fires are being reported every ten or fifteen minutes." He pointed to the corner of the room. "They start southwest of here and circle to the northeast, across the southern end of Pierce and up the old highway. DPS troopers are trying to find whoever's starting the fires."

"It's him," Maris said. "I bet the computer sent a signal to his pager notifying him that the house was entered. He's running but stopping every few miles to start another fire. He wants us tied up fighting fires."

Ralph listened intently to the radio. "Jeff reports that the wind is driving a major grass fire straight at us. They can send only one truck to help us because of the fires close to town. He says we need to move all of the vehicles back except for one."

"I'll help you," Wayne said. "I'm calling DPS and telling them to have the helicopter pick up the bomb squad and get them here — pronto."

Sally held her radio close to her ear. She whispered to Maris, "It's even worse than Ralph makes it sound. Jeff's having to drive several miles to the north to get back here."

"We can't wait around for the bomb squad," Maris said, picking up the cutting torch. "You better go help move the cars."

"I'm not leaving you to get blown up alone. You know how to use that thing?"

"You bet." Maris pulled on the goggles Wayne left by the torch next to the flint striker. "Don't you?"

"No."

"Don't worry. I won't tell." Maris grinned as she adjusted the gas. When she flicked the starter, a spark arched to the gas jet and the torch came to life. Adjusting the flame, she turned to the steel door.

It seemed to take forever before the lock fell to the charred floor. She kicked it to the side and cut off the torch. Sally handed her a rag and a screwdriver to slip through the handle on the door. "Fire's advancing rapidly. While you were working, I cut off all of the electricity to the house. It might help if any of his devices rely on it for the trigger mechanism."

It might, Maris thought, but she suspected that if he was a very sophisticated bomber, they'd already be dead. The light bulb was a slick, simple trick, although activating it with the computer was a nice touch. She pulled away the metal bar and tugged on the door. The door didn't budge. "Son-of-a-bitch must have warped from the fire."

Sally crowded in beside her and they pulled together. Maris pushed against the doorframe with her foot to gain more leverage. Every muscle in her body strained against the door before she felt it give. Slowly, it slid six inches, then swung free throwing Maris off balance and knocking Sally to the ground.

A surreal wailing escaped from the dark opening as the acrid odor of urine and blood assailed them. Tripping over the torch, Maris stumbled through the open doorway into a large bunker. Sally held a spotlight over her shoulder and Maris froze. Suspended from the ceiling and held against the wall with chains and nylon cords attached to a leather harness, Lisa Anderson twisted, naked, in mid-air. Blood ran down the inside of her white, bruised and cut thighs and dripped into a growing pool on the floor. She screamed and her eyes rolled wildly, then, her body went limp and she stopped struggling.

She looked at Maris and for a brief moment, her dark, tortured eyes cleared. She said, "Let me die."

Wayne thrust his six-foot-five, bulky frame past Sally. "We've got to get the fuck out of here," he said. Seeing Lisa, he stopped in his tracks. Lisa jerked her head up and began screaming. Thrashing and twisting, she clawed at the harness in frantic efforts to escape.

Maris sprinted across the concrete floor. Waving at Wayne, she said, "Get out of sight. She's afraid of you." She gently touched Lisa's leg. "Lisa, you're safe now. We're here to help you."

Wayne backed out of the room and Lisa stopped struggling. "Stop the pain," she whispered. She shifted her weight against the leather and nylon restraints, causing the chains to rattle, and Maris saw the cuts on her breasts, stomach and neck for the first time. Burn marks covered her hips, buttocks and thighs. Maris looked around the room for something to help support Lisa's weight.

"Lord almighty, how are we going to get her down from there?" Sally said before a fit of coughing racked her body. For the first time Maris noticed the smoke pouring into the bunker from the door.

Maris encircled Lisa at the hips, relieving some of the weight from the restraints that were cutting her flesh. "I'll hold her while you cut the ropes and harness off of her. We need the torch to cut the chains."

Sally nodded. Wayne tried to enter the room with the torch and Lisa bucked and twisted in Maris's arms. He retreated. "Start the torch for Sally and hand it to her."

"Keep him away from me," Lisa wailed.

Wayne gave Sally the torch. Balancing precariously on a stool, she quickly cut through the chains and the nylon ropes. The ends of the ropes melted and burst into flames but soon burned out. As gently as possible, they lowered Lisa to the concrete floor. Wayne tossed a blanket and some towels and a sheet into the room. Maris pressed a towel between Lisa's legs, hoping to slow the bleeding. They covered Lisa with the blanket.

"Die . . . want to . . . die," she cried weakly. Maris glanced around the room. Knives, a stun gun, a cattle prod, dildos of various sizes and knotted whips cluttered a table against the wall. A freezer stood in one corner and an oak display case, beautifully polished, was filled with women's high-heeled shoes, all black. A machete leaned against the corner wall. A dull gray meat hook bolted into the wall caught her attention. The autopsy photographs of the unexplained wound in Theresa Eastin's side flashed through her mind. She shuddered. At least Lisa had been spared that.

"We can't wait for an ambulance," Wayne said. "I'll get another blanket to use as a stretcher."

"Shoot me. The pain is . . ." Her voice trailed off. Sweat glistened on her brow and she clenched her teeth. Her body racked in a spasm that scared Maris.

Wayne pitched a blanket into the room. "The goddamn fire is on the back wall and spreading quickly. They've got a fire truck spraying water on the house and the propane tank. The son-of-a-bitch could blow any minute. If the fire gets any hotter, they'll have to pull out to keep the truck from burning."

"She's fading in and out of consciousness. I think she's losing too much blood," Maris said as she and Sally lifted the limp body onto the blanket.

Lisa's head jerked, and she screamed, "No, get away from me." Her body went slack. She drew rapid, shallow gasps of air.

"How much longer?" Wayne shouted between coughs. "A fireman's standing by with a pickup. When we get to the porch, he'll back up to it. He couldn't wait there. The tires were smoking."

"Coming," Maris called out. They rose with the makeshift stretcher and Sally backed through the metal doorframe into the closet. Following Sally into the smoke-filled computer room, Maris jumped when flames licked through the broken window. Occasionally a flicker could be seen lapping around a loose board on the hardwood floor. She felt the heat through the soles of her shoes. Lisa groaned. "She's bleeding a lot," Maris said as Wayne and Ralph each grabbed a side of the blanket when they reached the hallway. Sally cursed, dodging a falling chunk of ceiling.

Stepping on the porch, Maris gasped. Thick smoke obscured the sun and turned late afternoon into night. Fire could be seen in every direction. The Pierce volunteer firemen, conceding the house now that the occupants were almost out, backed the truck onto the road and fed a steady stream of water in the path of the Chevrolet pickup that sped backwards toward them. Maris felt the heat on her face, making her scar tingle. She coughed and tried to see through tearing eyes. She saw only dim images of Ralph, Sally and Wayne and heard them coughing. She heard the tailgate on the pickup drop and was drawn forward when Sally stepped back into the truck. A board gave way and Maris's left leg plunged through a gaping hole filled with fire and smoke. Dropping her hand to the porch, she caught herself, burning her palm. Ralph and Wayne grabbed her end with only a mild jolt to Lisa and lowered the blanket to the bed of the pickup. Maris scrambled upright, slapping burning embers on the cuffs of her coveralls. When she put weight on her left ankle, she stumbled and almost fell again. Ralph grabbed her arm and half carried her to the back of the pickup. She collapsed into the bed as the truck accelerated, forcing them to grab the side. The firemen pulled in the heavy water hose and the fire truck fell in behind the pickup.

An explosion rocked both trucks and Maris felt a rush of hot air slap her cheeks. Portions of metal rained down on the road behind them.

"Propane tank must have gone," Wayne said. "Are you hurt, Maris?"

"My left ankle is a little sore. I'll be fine."

The truck pulled into a command post two miles from the farmhouse. Maris's Ford pickup, to her relief, was parked near Wayne and Sally's cars. As the truck came to a halt, a CareFlite helicopter landed and two paramedics leapt out and grabbed a stretcher. They lifted Lisa over the side of the pickup to the waiting flight crew who secured her to the stretcher and raced to the helicopter. Maris saw a nurse starting an IV as the helicopter left the ground. A pool of blood glistened on the bed of the pickup where it had soaked through the blanket.

"I hope she makes it," Maris said. Thick smoke soon hid the helicopter from sight.

Chapter Nineteen

Southern Pierce county was in chaos and the search for Donnie Wade Baker was swept aside in the confusion. Every officer and any other available hand joined the fire fighters in attacking the advancing flames or in evacuating people from houses and businesses in the path of the raging inferno. Maris limped around the command post trying to walk off the pain in her ankle, hoping to help fight the fires, but it was useless. With the ankle swelling rapidly, feeling searing pain at each step, she suspected it was cracked or broken. She found tape and an ace bandage in a first aid kit and wrapped it. Although reluctant to leave, she knew she could become a liability on her bad ankle if the fire advanced too rapidly. So far, no human lives had perished but countless livestock and wild animals were lost and property damage was high. She left without protest when Wayne insisted she go home.

Tired, the constant pain in her ankle sapping her energy, Maris sighed with relief when she finally came to the exit for her neighborhood. She jumped when her pager vibrated in her pocket and grabbed it, surprised to see the number for the task force office. She dialed the car phone and it was answered on the first ring.

"Maris, where are you?" Viola demanded, panic in her voice.

"Almost home, what's wrong?"

"Whatever you do, don't go home. I just checked our e-mail and there's a message for you posted two hours ago. It said, 'By the time you get home, dyke, even the dog will be dead.' Don't go home. I'm calling Allen P.D. right now." The line went dead.

Maris's stomach twisted and her chest tightened, making it almost impossible to draw air. Shoving the accelerator to the floor, she dropped the telephone and gripped the steering wheel with white knuckles. Not go home, like hell, what if Lauren was already home? She knew she was closer than the police, and her Smith and Wesson .38 was under the seat. Damn it, why hadn't she bought or traded for one of the semi-automatic pistols — either a Sig 228 like Lauren carried or one of the .40 calibers everyone was excited about. But she was a good shot and she could make do with the little .38 and its five jacketed hollowpoint bullets. Careening onto her street, she narrowly missed a white Ford Crown Victoria parked on the right side of the road three houses from hers. In the driveway, behind Lauren's Firebird, stood a beige Ford Explorer.

Screeching the pickup to a halt, Maris threw the transmission into park and paused to retrieve the .38 revolver. She stumbled across the sidewalk. Wincing, she tried to run to the open door, but her ankle gave way. She fell hard on the concrete sidewalk. Struggling against panic, she scrambled to her feet and limped as fast as possible, half-dragging her left leg. "Don't let her be dead. Please, God, don't let her be dead," she mumbled as she reached the door.

Flattening herself against the wall, she inched her way inside. She crept into the foyer, holding the revolver in position to fire. Straining to see, she willed her smoke-strained eyes to adjust from the bright sunshine to the interior darkness. She almost tripped over Earnhardt. He lay prone across the threshold to the living room. Blood spread from a wound in his side. Two shots rang out from the direction of the guest bedroom. Using the wall for support, she raced as quickly as her ankle allowed. Turning toward the sound of gunshots, ready to fire if necessary, she saw Barbara Shelton grappling with a heavy-set white male for control of a Glock semi-auto. Maris recognized him immediately. He was nude from the waist down and his fat, pale legs jiggled as he fought with Barbara.

Lauren lay on the bed behind them. Her bright red fingernails glistened under the light from the overhead ceiling fan and her hands strained against the handcuffs that held her to the headboard. Her

black dress was torn to expose her pale breasts and
the hem was bunched at her waist. She was nude
from the waist down except for black shoes with two
inch heels that had ripped the bedspread. Pantyhose
knotted in a noose around her neck were ready to be
loosened or tightened at Donnie Wade's pleasure. The
bedroom was in wild disarray with shoes and shoe
boxes piled on the carpet, on the bureau and around
the bed.

Maris felt like she had crouched in the doorway
for minutes, but she knew it had been only a second
or two. So far neither of the combatants realized she
was there. Willing her bad ankle to support her, she
took three long strides into the room and in one
swift, fluid movement cocked the pistol, placed it a
couple of inches from Donnie Wade's head and pulled
the trigger. The little .38 was deafening in the small
bedroom. Maris swore his eyes registered surprise
when the bullet hit but awareness, if any, was fleet-
ing. The bullet did its job and exited out of the other
side of his head in a cloud of blood and bone fragments. He fell on the bed across Lauren's waist.
Maris's ankle gave way and she stumbled to one
knee.

Regaining her footing, she screamed, "Get the
fuck away from her." And, with all the strength she
could muster, she grabbed his shirt and jerked him
off of Lauren. Although he weighed at least two
hundred pounds, she flung him backwards against the
wall where he slumped into a semi-prone position. In
rage, Maris squeezed the trigger on the .38 four more
times. Four hollowpoint bullets tore through his white
shirt. Very little blood trickled from the entry
wounds. His torso slipped sideways and blood stained

the wall. Maris threw the gun at him as hard as she could. It hit him in the chest, bounced once and landed on the floor near the bed.

"Maris." Lauren sobbed.

Maris's stomach churned when her attention turned to Lauren and what he might have done. She searched for the key to the handcuffs and found them in his left pocket. With trembling hands, she unlocked them. Struggling to loosen the pantyhose, she opened her pocket knife with shaking hands and cut the nylons away. Lauren's wrists were cut and bruised. A red, raw ring circled her neck. For the first time, Maris noticed a lump, purple around the edges, on the upper left side of her head.

Lauren gripped her in a crushing embrace. Maris felt hot, damp tears on her neck and swallowed hard. She gently touched Lauren's tangled red hair. Her knee bumped into a pair of pliers, knocking them to the floor. Gently, she pushed Lauren away from her, checking for injuries. The significance of the pliers hit her when she saw the ugly red marks around each of Lauren's nipples. Dark bruises, shaped with the ridge pattern of the pliers, marred her breasts. She pulled Lauren to her.

With her head buried against Maris's neck and shoulder, Lauren said, "After the airport shuttle dropped me off, I unlocked the front door. I thought I heard the phone ringing and ran inside, leaving my suitcase on the porch. Earnhardt was dancing to go out so I went with him. I waited until he was finished and brought him back inside. As I unlocked the front door and stepped out to get my bag, he blindsided me. I was surprised and never reached for my gun. How could I let this happen? I'm supposed to be trained. Earnhardt, oh my God, Earnhardt, Maris, I'm so sorry."

"Hush, hush, none of this is your fault. Thank God you're alive." Maris fought to maintain her composure. "I don't think I could survive losing you."

She had forgotten Barbara was there until she felt a hand on her shoulder. "We need to call the police, DPS. Get help for Lauren."

"How bad are you hurt, baby?" Maris asked.

"I may have lost consciousness. He took me into the bedroom . . . our bedroom. I remember him tearing off my clothes. He cuffed my hands and tied the pantyhose around my neck. He dragged me through the bedroom and bathroom. He had the pair of pliers in his hip pocket and found the nail polish in the bathroom closet —" Her voice cracked and Maris felt the sobs shake her body.

"Barbara, page Wayne Coffey. Allen P.D. is en route." Maris told her the pager number.

After dialing his number, Barbara returned to the foot of the bed. "Can I get you anything, honey?"

"My robe, please."

The telephone rang and Barbara answered it. Maris heard her muffled voice but couldn't make out the words. She came back into the room carrying Lauren's maroon robe and a glass of water. Maris steadied the glass for her.

Lauren said, almost whispering, "He made me paint my nails while he masturbated. He couldn't stay hard. That's when he began to use the pliers. He called me a stupid fucking bitch. Said we were all so stupid. He could only get hard when he was hurting me. He dragged me into the back bedroom. He relaxed the tension on the pantyhose around my neck and I said, 'I thought your thing was women in high heels.' I pointed to the closet. He was ecstatic when he discovered all of my shoes. He began rifling through them tossing shoes and boxes everywhere until he found these heels. Then he went through my clothes until he came to this black dress and made me put it on. I hoped he'd forget to recuff me, but he didn't. He ripped the dress and used the pliers some more. He forced my legs apart and took a couple of twists in the panty hose. I closed my eyes. I felt him touching me and Barbara shouted for him to freeze. He leapt off of the bed and charged her. She fired two shots but missed. I think he shoved her arm aside." Lauren looked up at Barbara. "Thank God you came when you did."

"I heard the task force was trying to get a warrant and thought I might catch Maris before she left to meet the team." Barbara stared at her hands. "I came to beg for the information . . . to try anything to find out who the suspect was and where they were running the warrant. I envisioned shooting him as they led him into the jail. The front door was open and I saw the dog. I heard screams." She started crying for the first time. "I told him to freeze but he charged me. He was on me by the time I fired the first shot. I must have hesitated." Maris looked up and saw two holes in the ceiling. "I'm crying because . . . if Maris hadn't gotten here when she did, I don't know what would have happened. I'm sorry for what he's done to you, to Cynthia and all of the others. For the pain he's caused. I'm sorry I'm not the one who killed him."

"I'm sorry that the bastard could only die once," Maris said. "It's not enough for all that he's done."

Lauren sighed. "Help me up. The police should be here soon. Let's check on Earnhardt." Maris took her elbow and helped her into the robe. Lauren tied it closed over the ripped black dress. Since Maris could barely walk, Barbara helped Lauren down the hall.

Earnhardt, Maris thought as she knelt beside him, we've been through so much together. Touching his side, she felt it barely rise and fall. His feet moved and he tried to raise his head. "He's still alive," she said.

"He fought so hard for me." Lauren wiped the tears from her eyes.

"Police!" yelled two uniformed Allen policemen as they lunged through the open door, nine-millimeter pistols drawn.

Maris pointed down the hallway. "It's over. The bastard is dead."

Barbara, dodging one of the bewildered officers as he raced down the hallway, returned with a towel. Gently, Maris wrapped the towel around Earnhardt and lifted him into her arms. She limped awkwardly toward the door as the second wave of police officers arrived. A female officer tried to stop Maris from leaving until she heard Earnhardt whimper. Sirens blaring, the officer drove Maris the short distance to the veterinary clinic. They were working frantically to save his life when the officer pulled Maris out of the waiting room and helped her to the squad car.

Chapter Twenty

Wayne, Sally and Ralph, smelling strongly of
smoke, arrived within an hour after Maris returned
from the vet's office. Wayne and an Allen P.D. detective took a simple statement from Lauren while
Ralph and another detective interviewed Maris at the
kitchen bar. They'd talk to Barbara after Sally drove
Maris and Lauren to Parkland Hospital in downtown
Dallas. Sally packed Lauren a change of clothes
before they left. The emergency room personnel were
kind and concerned and ushered Lauren into an
examination room immediately. Maris knew the

swelling in her shoe and elastic bandage had reached a dangerous point, but she stayed by Lauren's side until the doctor arrived. While they waited, she convinced Lauren of the necessity for a complete sexual assault examination even though she said Donnie Wade hadn't raped her. Although she and Sally didn't admit it to Lauren, they wanted to make sure he didn't complete the act while she was unconscious. Photographs were taken of her bruised breasts and the red, swollen abrasion on her head before they sent her to have her ribs X-rayed.

Maris wanted to be nearby when the doctor performed the pelvic examination, but a cagey emergency room nurse spotted her ankle and shoved her into a wheelchair for her own trip to X-ray. Luckily, the break was only partway through the bone and surgery was not necessary. The E.R. doctor set it in a blue cast, although Maris really wanted camouflage, and told her not to walk on it. He referred her to an orthopedic doctor for follow-up treatment. A nurse cleaned and bandaged the minor burn on her hand while she waited for them to bring her crutches and a prescription for pain medication.

Passing Sally, who was on the phone at the nurse's counter, Maris clumsily swung into Lauren's examination room on her new crutches. Clutching the front of a paper gown, Lauren sat on the side of the table while two FBI agents stood, one on each side of her, taking notes.

One, a gray-headed man about fifty-five, smiled gently and said, "We'll call tomorrow and check on you. Anything you need, call me — anything." He gave Maris an encouraging pat on the shoulder as he left the room and whispered, "Good shooting."

"What did the doctor say?" Maris asked while she helped Lauren dress in the running suit Sally had packed for her.

"I have a cracked rib. No concussion. My bruises should be fine in time, but they want to do a mammogram in a month to check for anything unusual. We've done photographs and documented everything. I can go as soon as they bring me a prescription for pain pills."

"I'm sorry, honey. After everything that's happened, I should have known he'd do this. As soon as we got Lisa out of the house, I should have come home."

"I won't blame myself if you won't blame yourself." Lauren smiled wearily.

"Do you want to go to a hotel or should I call Kathy — see if we can stay there tonight?"

"I want to go home."

"Are you sure? It'll still be a mess."

"He's not running us out of our home."

Maris hugged her. She was pleased Lauren felt that way.

Sally returned to the room carrying a white paper sack with Lauren's tattered black dress and black heels, and another bag with the sexual assault kit. "We finished here?" she asked.

"Soon as they bring Lauren her prescription. What have you heard about Lisa Anderson?"

"She came out of emergency surgery an hour ago. I called the waiting room and spoke to her lover, Vicki. They did extensive surgery to repair tears in her vagina. She lost her spleen and gall bladder and has two broken ribs, a broken wrist and a cracked vertebra in her neck. She's in pretty bad shape, but the doctors are optimistic. The next forty-eight hours are critical."

News of Lisa's rescue, the assault on Lauren, and Donnie Wade's death had spread rapidly, and about a dozen reporters waited outside the emergency room. Sally ran the gauntlet of shouting reporters and pulled her black Chevrolet Caprice up to the curb while Lauren and Maris waited inside the door.

When she returned, Maris said, "Get Lauren through the crowd. Take care of her. I'll be fine."

Even before the emergency room door opened, the reporters started tossing questions at them. Hospital security helped block a path for them, and Sally rushed Lauren to the car. Maris, fighting the crutches, followed a short distance behind as quickly as she could. Reporters hurled questions at her: Who shot Donnie Wade Baker? Was he the serial killer? Was the FBI agent raped? What did the torture room look like? How is Lisa Anderson? Is it true all of his victims are lesbians?

Maris was acquainted with the reporter who blocked her path. He mistook her recognition as encouragement and shouted, "Is it true that you shot Donnie Wade Baker four times at point-blank range after he was disabled with a severe head wound?"

Anger flashed in Maris. Someone was already leaking information. Maris could smell cheap whiskey on his breath when he stepped closer.

"Why did you keep shooting him? Were you afraid he'd live? Was it to cover up evidence, to protect someone else, to avoid a trial, to cover up task force mistakes? Aren't you guilty of overkill?"

Maris stopped in her tracks and glared at the reporter. "Since I didn't have a wooden stake or a

222

silver bullet, I had to make do with five little ol' thirty-eight hollowpoints. But it's impossible to over- kill a monster."

Sally shouldered the reporter out of the way. He threw his cigarette to the ground and said, "What did those dyke man-haters expect dressing the way they did? Sexy heels and red nail polish. They were asking for trouble."

Anger exploded inside Maris. Sally didn't move fast enough and Maris slipped past her. Dropping her crutches, she delivered an elbow-jarring right hook and felt a surge of satisfaction as the reporter's nose cartilage gave under her fist. He stumbled backwards. Maris, forgetting her left ankle was in a cast, pur- sued. Falling to the ground, she bounced up. Hopping on one foot, she shouted, "Get up, you son-of-a- bitch!" Sally stuck a crutch under each of her arms and whirled her in the direction of the car.

"I'll file charges, you bitch. I have lots of wit- nesses."

"No, you don't, you idiot," another reporter said, leading the pack away from their downed comrade. "Your bosses find out about that comment and you're history. Every feminist and gay and lesbian organi- zation in the world will be on your ass."

The house was in better shape than Maris expec- ted. When her former co-workers from the DPS lab finished their investigation, Wayne called in a bio- hazards clean-up company to remove the blood in the house. He went to a twenty-four-hour pharmacy to fill their prescriptions for pain medication while Sally put clean sheets and blankets on the bed. She waited with Maris and Lauren until the clean-up was finished. When everyone was finally gone, Lauren supported Maris on one side and they walked through the house. The boxes, clothing and shoes still littered the floor, but the bedding was gone. The carpet was damp and a four-foot-square section of sheetrock had been cut out of the wall.

"I feel like I'm sleepwalking," Lauren said, resting her head on Maris's shoulder.

"That's normal after something like this. I miss Earnhardt."

"I hope he's doing well." Lauren squeezed her waist. "I can't wait another minute to shower."

Maris watched patiently while Lauren scrubbed with soap and water two, then three times. Letting the water flow over her battered body, she stood in the shower until it was clear the hot water was almost gone. Realizing what she had done, Lauren burst into tears and apologized. Balancing on one foot, Maris held her and dried her tears. "Don't worry about it. By the time you get me undressed and put a trash bag over my cast, we'll have plenty of hot water." They were both thankful that Sally had made their bed, even though a faint odor of smoke clung to the covers.

Waking alone in the dark, Maris struggled out of bed to look for Lauren. Her ankle ached as she swung the heavy cast to the edge of the bed and reached for her crutches. She found Lauren in the back bedroom, swaying unsteadily as she picked up her shoes and tossed them into a black trash bag. Tears ran down her cheek, soaking her nightshirt.

Maris swung in front of her and, leaning on her crutches, gently took her by the arms. Taking the trash bag from her hand, Maris let in fall to the floor. Collapsing on the bare mattress, she pulled Lauren down next to her and placed an arm around her shoulders. "Honey, why are you doing this?"

"He touched them."

"I know, but there's no need to throw them all away."

"You were right. I have more shoes than anyone needs."

"Thank God you had them. It gave him something to do until Barbara got here. Let's forget about picking this up for now." Maris dropped her arm to Lauren's waist and pulled her closer. Lauren stiffened and jerked away. "I'm sorry. Did I hurt your ribs?" Maris asked, releasing her immediately.

"I'm sore all over." Lauren started crying again. "Damn it, why can't I get control of myself?"

"You're hurt and tired. You need some time to recover."

"What if I don't recover? I mean, I've heard stories. What if, what about . . . what'll you do if I can't stand for you to touch my breasts again?"

Maris shrugged. "I don't know — play with your ears."

"Oh, God, not that," Lauren said, almost smiling. "You'll end up with a bloody nose again." The hint of a smile faded. "I can't stop thinking about him. Every time I close my eyes, I see him."

"We'll get through this, honey. Let's go back to bed." Maris pulled herself up with the crutches and helped Lauren up. Concerned at the way Lauren hugged herself as she walked down the hallway, Maris followed, carefully threading her way through the overturned boxes, scattered shoes and the black trash bag. By the time Maris settled in next to her, Lauren was in bed with the covers tucked tightly around her.

Chapter Twenty-one

The special agents from the Investigative Support Unit at Quantico called Lauren on Thursday, the first day after the assault, and invited her to go with them to interview Donnie Wade Baker's sister on Saturday. They hoped the additional information would help them develop more accurate sex offender psychological profiles. Lauren hesitated before accepting their invitation, but Maris urged her to go. She hoped it was the right thing to do. Maris knew she couldn't expect a full emotional recovery after only three days, but she hoped it might help Lauren win back some of her self confidence and battle her depression.

That first morning had been bad. Lauren slept and cried, slept and cried. Maris couldn't do or say anything to help her, and she refused to let her call anyone else. While she slept, Maris called David, Lauren's brother, and told him what happened but decided he should wait to talk to Lauren. Sally, Wayne and a detective from Allen P.D. came by before lunch with the good news that the Collin county district attorney refused to file charges against Maris and would recommend that the grand jury no-bill her in the death of Donnie Wade Baker. They had Maris and Lauren reread their statements and make corrections and additions as needed. Afterwards Lauren slept four hours straight before rising to eat with Maris. She'd been afraid to leave Lauren alone for very long at a time, and it made it difficult to work in the lab. When she did work, the crutches cut her efficiency in half. If Earnhardt had been there, she could have left him in with Lauren and cracked the door to the lab. He'd have let her know if Lauren needed anything. Maris missed him.

Although reluctant to leave, she'd slipped out of the house to see him once around four while she was asleep. Lauren went with her the second day. He seemed so sick that Maris wondered if she was wrong to try to save him. She didn't want him to suffer, but she didn't want to put him to sleep if there was a chance. The vet said to wait another day or two.

Saturday morning, the third day after the assault, Lauren left to meet the agents from Quantico. As soon as she was out of the driveway, Maris discarded her crutches in disgust and practiced walking on the cast. It hurt like hell, but she decided she could endure it long enough to complete her intended task. At the lumberyard, the employees loaded lumber and other supplies for her. Her real problem was unloading the material when she got home, but her balance improved with practice. The burn on her left hand was almost more irritating.

Before starting her project, she covered her cast in a black trash bag and wrapped duct tape around the top of it to keep out the sawdust. Starting with the closet in the middle bedroom, the junk room, she moved up the top shelf and clothes rod and added a vertical divider that separated a portion for dresses and longer articles of clothing. On the other side of the divider, she added a second rod partway to the floor that created another row for shorter items. When she finished, almost all of Lauren's hanging clothes fit in the middle bedroom closet.

It seemed strange to work without Earnhardt darting underfoot and she missed him terribly as she cleaned and polished the scattered shoes and attempted to return them to the appropriate shoebox. She used metal shelf-hangers to add three rows of horizontal shelves. This was the largest closet in the duplex, running almost the full length of the bedroom wall. When she finished, it was three-quarters full of neatly arranged shoes and shoeboxes with space left over to add a small filing cabinet later for Lauren's personal papers. By the time she vacuumed the floors to remove the sawdust, her ankle, swollen and aching, pounded inside her cast. Despite the pain, she was pleased. The reorganized closets created a sense of permanence for Lauren's possessions. To complete the clean-up, Maris ordered new carpet and curtains and scheduled an acquaintance to repair the wall and paint the room.

After putting away the last tool, she collapsed into her recliner with a cold Miller Lite. Halfway through the beer, she heard Lauren's key in the door. She took one look at Maris, curled up her nose and said, "What have you been doing?"

Maris thought her color was better and her eyes sharper. She struggled painfully to her feet and reached for Lauren's shoulder. "Come here, girl. I have a surprise for you."

"I have two surprises for you."

"Well, come with me first. This won't take very long."

"I hope not. One of my surprises can't wait very long. God, you're getting sweat and sawdust all over me."

Lauren followed her into the guest bedroom and froze. Her gaze first went to the clean but stained spot on the floor and the hole in the wall. Looking for the shoes, she opened the louvered closet doors and gasped. "How did you do this with your broken ankle?" The tears began to fall and Maris limped over to her.

"I thought you'd like it."

"I do like it. I can't believe you did it for me."

"It'll take about a week, but eventually I'll get the wall fixed, paint the room and have new carpet installed. I think we'll also rearrange the furniture. Look in the middle bedroom."

Lauren ran ahead while Maris limped slowly down

the hallway, using the wall for support. She heard the closet door open and close before Lauren rushed out of the bedroom and threw her arms around her. Maris hugged her tightly and felt her wince from pain. Lauren backed off a little but didn't stop kissing her.

"I thought you were afraid I'd get you dirty," Maris teased.

"Thank you, lover, but you shouldn't have done it with your broken ankle. Go sit in your chair while I get your surprise."

Maris dropped into her recliner and finished the last half of her beer. She heard a whimpering sound and turned to look down the foyer. Lauren gently lowered Earnhardt to the floor. Maris dropped to the carpet in front of her chair and hugged him when he limped to her and barked weakly. He enthusiastically licked her face before sinking to floor next to her with one paw on her leg.

"Earnhardt, my friend, I thought we'd lost you." She swallowed, not wanting to cry.

"The doctor confirmed that he had a concussion from a kick to the head and was stabbed, but luckily the knife missed his heart and lungs. I stopped and begged to bring him home. The vet said he had improved a lot today and agreed to let me have him. But no ball-playing for three weeks. Keep him inside and as quiet as possible and make sure he finishes his antibiotics. The vet says he should be fine. By the way, lover, did you read the paper today?"

"No, I've worked on the closets all day."

Lauren dropped cross-legged on the other side of Maris. She looped her arm under Maris's elbow and reached across her to pet Earnhardt. "Your comment about the wooden stake and the silver bullet has made you quite a celebrity, especially after you slugged the reporter. Why didn't you tell me about your impromptu press conference?"

Maris laughed but said nothing.

Lauren smiled at her and stroked Earnhardt. "I stopped by the hospital on my way back. Lisa is out of intensive care. She may get to go home in three or four days. The agents from Quantico and I will wait until then to interview her more completely. She told her lover, Vicki, that she remembers you coming into the cave — as she calls it. She thought you were an angel sent from God to take her soul and end her suffering."

"First time I've ever been mistaken for an angel of mercy."

"She still thinks you are. Wayne told her you were the one most responsible for the leads that led them to Donnie Wade. She also knows that you're the one who killed him. She's glad he's dead and can't hurt anyone else. And that there'll be no trial. She wanted you to have this. Vicki had a friend make it."

When Lauren handed Maris the envelope, she felt a hard lump in the center, almost pushing through the white paper.

She tore it open and dumped the contents into her hand. A silver bullet with a silver chain through a hole in its base fell out. "This is really nice, but it was a team effort."

Lauren squeezed Maris's arm. "Yes, but you're the one who brought it to an end."

Maris dropped the chain over her head and fingered the silver bullet. It felt cool, solid against her chest. Putting an arm around Lauren, she grinned. "Thank God for Smith and Wesson."

A few of the publications of
THE NAIAD PRESS, INC.
P.O. Box 10543   Tallahassee, Florida 32302
Phone (850) 539-5965
Toll-Free Order Number: 1-800-533-1973
Mail orders welcome. Please include 15% postage.
Write or call for our free catalog which also features an
incredible selection of lesbian videos.

POSSESSIONS by Kaye Davis. 240 pp. 2nd Maris Middleton
Mystery.   ISBN 1-56280-192-9 $11.95

A QUESTION OF LOVE by Saxon Bennett. 204 pp. Every
woman is granted one great love.   ISBN 1-56280-205-4   11.95

RHYTHM TIDE by Frankie J. Jones. 160 pp.   . . . to desire
passionately and be passionately desired.   ISBN 1-56280-189-9   11.95

PENN VALLEY PHOENIX by Janet McClellan. 208 pp. 2nd
Tru North Mystery.   ISBN 1-56280-200-3   11.95

BY RESERVATION ONLY by Jackie Calhoun. 240 pp. A
chance for true happiness.   ISBN 1-56280-191-0   11.95

OLD BLACK MAGIC by Jaye Maiman. 272 pp. 9th Robin
Miller Mystery.   ISBN 1-56280-175-9   11.95

LEGACY OF LOVE by Marianne K. Martin. 240 pp. Women
will do anything for her . . .   ISBN 1-56280-184-8   11.95

LETTING GO by Ann O'Leary. 160 pp. Laura, at 39, in love
with 23-year-old Kate.   ISBN 1-56280-183-X   11.95

LADY BE GOOD edited by Barbara Grier and Christine Cassidy.
288 pp. Erotic stories by Naiad Press authors.   ISBN 1-56280-180-5   14.95

CHAIN LETTER by Claire McNab. 288 pp. 9th Carol Ashton
mystery.   ISBN 1-56280-181-3   11.95

NIGHT VISION by Laura Adams. 256 pp. Erotic fantasy romance
by "famous" author.   ISBN 1-56280-182-1   11.95

These are just a few of the many Naiad Press titles — we are the oldest and
largest lesbian/feminist publishing company in the world. We also offer an
enormous selection of lesbian video products. Please request a complete
catalog. We offer personal service; we encourage and welcome direct mail
orders from individuals who have limited access to bookstores carrying our
publications.